CLOSE ENCOUNTERS OF THE WITCHY KIND

A WICKED WITCHES OF THE MIDWEST FANTASY
BOOK SIX

AMANDA M. LEE

WINCHESTERSHAW PUBLICATIONS

Copyright © 2018 by Amanda M. Lee

All rights reserved.

No part of this book may be reproduced in any form or by any electronic or mechanical means, including information storage and retrieval systems, without written permission from the author, except for the use of brief quotations in a book review.

❦ Created with Vellum

ALIEN INSPIRATION

" Why would aliens choose to visit Hemlock Cove? We have a pewter unicorn store. That should convince them that we're devoid of intelligent life.
Bay on the odds of aliens landing in town

ONE

A LONG TIME AGO, IN AN INN FAR, FAR AWAY ... .

"I think you should put a big portrait of me right here, so when you're working and feeling lonely you can simply stare at the wall and see the most influential person in your life watching you."

I looked up from where I sat cross-legged on the floor — I was sorting through folders and documents for my new filing cabinet — and graced my cousin Thistle with a dark look. Her hair, a bright shade of pink that was more Pepto-Bismol than perky, was so bright it clashed with the lavender color I'd picked for the walls of my new office.

"Why would I possibly want a portrait of you?" I asked, legitimately curious.

"I just told you. I'm the most influential person in your life."

Either she was delusional or trying to goad me. I leaned toward the latter. "Uh-huh." I turned back to my organizational efforts. "I'm almost done. Once I finish with the files, The Whistler offices will be completely reorganized and all memory of Brian Kelly will be gone."

"I bet you can't wait for that," my other cousin, Clove, enthused.

Her dark brown hair hung past her shoulders. She was the shortest member of our terrible threesome, so she often felt the need to talk loudly to overcompensate. Today was no exception. "I know I would be throwing a party to get the stink off the building."

"I think that would be a little juvenile."

Thistle made a face. "Since when does that matter? We were taught how to be juvenile delinquents by the very best. Speaking of that, have you considered calling Aunt Tillie to do a cleansing of this place? I know the idea of letting her inside goes against your survival instincts, but in this one instance she might be some help."

That sounded unlikely. My great-aunt was the sort to shorten my lifespan, not increase it. Sure, she was elderly and helped raise us and I loved her. She was also nutty, vindictive and occasionally so nasty that I preferred hiding from her. Yes, she's just that powerful. Still, I got along better with her than Thistle. If Thistle was suggesting that I invite her inside my new business offices — yes, I, Bay Winchester, am officially a business owner — then she must have sensed something even worse than I'd initially envisioned.

"Why would I possibly invite Aunt Tillie here?" I challenged. "She'll try to take over the decorating process."

Thistle wrinkled her nose as she looked at the bare walls. "She couldn't possibly make things worse."

I scowled. "I'm still deciding how I want to decorate. It's a big decision. There's nothing wrong with taking my time and really putting some thought into decorating."

Thistle rolled her eyes so hard she gave the impression that she was tilting to the side. "Whatever."

"No, really. I agree with Bay," Clove argued, shaking her head. "This is her space now. She deserves the right to decorate it how she wants."

I beamed at my cousin. "Thank you, Clove."

Clove returned the smile. "You're welcome, Bay."

"Oh, both of you are total pains in my backside," Thistle complained loudly. "Why don't you back up the mutual admiration train and actually look at this analytically? This office is purple —

which I like — but the walls are empty. How can you work in a room that doesn't have any art to inspire you?"

Sadly, she had a point. I was so excited when the opportunity to buy Hemlock Cove's only newspaper arose — I grew up in town, so when I decided to be a journalist I cut my teeth at the facility with the former owner, William Kelly — I couldn't see beyond signing the papers and closing the deal. Part of me believed I would never really own the newspaper and William's weaselly grandson Brian would find a way to screw me out of what I so desperately wanted. So when the papers went through I was surprised. Now, several weeks in, I was starting to wrap my head around some of it ... although other parts remained elusive.

"I'm going to put art up in here," I repeated, finding my voice. "I want it to be good art, though. As for feeling inspired, let's be honest, this is a small town. Last week's top story was about the hybrid roses Brad Tolliver is planting in his greenhouse to liven up the summer festivals. Some things can't be livened up no matter how inspired you are."

Clove snickered as Thistle made an exaggerated face.

"I saw photographs of those roses," Clove volunteered in an effort to change the subject. Ever the peacemaker, she was often uncomfortable when Thistle and I started going at it. "They're called rainbow roses, and they're amazing. They're, like, eight different colors. They're so cool."

"I've seen photographs online," I acknowledged. "I showed them to Landon and told him the next time he wants to buy me something to get me in the mood he should look in that direction."

In addition to being my live-in boyfriend, Landon Michaels is an FBI agent. He was based out of the Traverse City office, but he'd recently convinced his boss that moving away from the office (and in with me) would improve his productivity. I wasn't sure he would actually be able to carry through on that promise, but sharing a roof with him was more fun than I'd expected. Things were going well. Between my new living arrangements and becoming my own boss, I didn't have much to complain about. But I'm suspicious and cynical by nature so that naturally means I believe something bad is doomed to happen.

What? That's simply how I roll. If things are good for too long, I understand that they will go bad ... and quickly. That's the natural order of things. As a witch — yes, I'm really a witch and can cast spells and talk to ghosts (amongst other things) — I have faith there's a natural order to the world. As part of that order, good must always follow bad. The universe is cyclical in nature. Things had been good for weeks, not a gray cloud in sight. That couldn't possibly last.

"Landon will buy you a bouquet of bacon before you get rainbow roses," Thistle argued. "His mind doesn't work to include girly things like that. Don't take it personally. He doesn't mean to be a dude."

"I'm not taking it personally." I meant it. I didn't need flowers. I was simply amazed by how pretty the rainbow roses were when I started researching them and couldn't stop myself from showing them to my boyfriend. "Landon helped me buy The Whistler. I definitely don't need flowers."

"That's true." Clove was always optimistic. Her eyes gleamed when I reminded her exactly how The Whistler fell into my hands. "He also threatened Brian with great bodily harm if he messed with you again. That's definitely better than flowers."

"Bay didn't need Landon to threaten Brian," Thistle reminded her. "We could've done it ourselves ... and been a lot more inventive."

She wasn't wrong. "I'm just glad he's gone. I thought for sure he'd come back and give me grief — or maybe try another trick like he did with the closing documents when he tried to screw me out of everything — but ultimately he just slunk away."

"You almost sound disappointed about that," Thistle noted. "Shouldn't you be happy that he took off the way he did?"

I wasn't sure how to answer the question. "I don't know," I said finally. "I expected more. It's not that I'm disappointed he left without saying goodbye or taking another parting shot. It's more that I can't believe he'd simply give up the way he did. And I'm worried he'll come back and try to pick another fight."

"I wouldn't worry about that," Clove said. "He's too afraid of Aunt

Tillie. He knows if he comes back to town that she'll castrate him — without anesthesia — so he really is doing himself a favor by letting this go. If he wanted to hold onto the newspaper, he shouldn't have tried to fire you the way he did."

The memory still smarted. "Yeah, well, let's talk about something else." I dusted my hands off on my jeans as I finished organizing. "That's it for the files." I placed the folders where they belonged in the horizontal cabinet and slid it shut. "My office is officially organized."

"And still devoid of art," Thistle groused, earning a dark look from me.

"The art will come," I fired back. "In fact, Landon and I are talking about going to that art show in Traverse City next weekend. It's supposed to be cool, with a lot of local artists. He suggested it."

"Because he knows an office without art is boring," Thistle pressed.

I was officially at my limit and could no longer rein in my temper. "Do you want me to take you outside and fill your mouth — which you can't seem to keep shut — with dirt? I'm willing to go that route for five minutes of peace."

Thistle didn't look particularly worried by my threat. "You're all talk. I'm not afraid of you."

"You should be."

"Pfft. Whatever." Thistle planted her hands on her hips as she looked around the room. "That art festival is probably a good idea. I'll talk to Landon and make sure he doesn't leave without forcing you to buy something."

"Why are you so bothered by the lack of art?" I challenged. "This isn't your space. You have a new house to decorate and a store you can gussy up whenever you want."

"First off, I can't gussy up the store whenever I want," Thistle argued. "I don't like that word, by the way. Gussy. It sounds like someone has eaten too many baked beans."

"Ugh. You're so gross." Clove flicked Thistle's ear as she passed behind her. "Do you always have to take it to a crass place?"

"I don't believe I'm talking to you," Thistle shot back. "As for the store, I share it with this one." She jerked a thumb in Clove's direction. "Our decorating tastes don't often mesh. Re-decorating the store is a bad idea because it will result in weeks of fighting."

"That's because you want to decorate with skulls. Your taste is morbid and annoying," Clove said.

"Sugar skulls," Thistle corrected. "I want sugar skulls. They're cute and awesome, and I'm convinced they'll draw more tourists into the store because everyone loves sugar skulls right now."

As loath as I was to admit Thistle was right, I always wanted their magic store to thrive, so I couldn't help agreeing with her. "You know, Thistle has a point," I supplied. "People do love sugar skulls ... and catrinas ... and anything Day of the Dead-ish. All that stuff is really big these days."

"Oh, I see you're on her side now." Clove's tone was withering and I recognized she was about to blow a gasket. "I see how things are."

"Oh, geez." I threw up my hands. "I give up. Let's go back to arguing about decorating this office."

Thistle snickered. "I think you should let me decorate."

"You have a new house to decorate," I reminded her. "Your boyfriend recognized you were weird enough to jump at the chance to move into a converted barn. I thought you were having a field day decorating that."

"I am." Thistle's eyes flashed with annoyance. "It's just ... Marcus doesn't always appreciate my decorating fervor. I was going to bring that up when we started talking about the store. That's why I said 'first off.' I had a second off. You distracted me and I forgot about it."

"Fine." I recognized the tone. Thistle was about to unleash one of her world-famous moods on us. It wasn't going to be pretty. I was familiar enough with her work to understand that. "Are you saying that Marcus won't let you decorate your own house?"

"It's not that," Thistle hedged. "It's just ... does Landon want to be involved in decorating the guesthouse with you? I mean ... is he interested in picking out art and knickknacks for the shelves?"

I tilted my head to the side, considering. "I don't know," I answered finally. "He doesn't push me on things like that. We just got all our stuff arranged how we like it. We haven't talked much about decorations."

"Well, Marcus and I have," Thistle said. "He wants to have a say in everything I put up. I think that's ludicrous. I'm an artist, for crying out loud. He's not an artist."

Marcus was so easygoing I had trouble imagining him doing anything of the sort. He tended to dote on Thistle, while still reining her in when she threatened to get out of control. He was the best possible match for her, and I couldn't imagine anyone else ever handling her as well as he did. "You're a store owner who dabbles as an artist," I corrected. "I've seen your work and it's beautiful. What doesn't Marcus want in the house?"

"I might have made a sculpture he doesn't like," Thistle admitted.

Oh, well, my interest was officially piqued. "What kind of sculpture?"

"Yeah, I want to know, too," Clove interjected, her eyes lighting with potential mayhem. She could sense when things were about to shift, and she was always looking for an edge in her ongoing battle with Thistle. "Spill."

"I thought he would like the sculpture," Thistle said. "I thought he would take one look at it and cry or something. Okay, maybe not cry. There was a chance for him to turn misty. That's how cool it was."

I was practically salivating. There was a reason she wasn't describing the sculpture. I had to know what it was. "And what did this cool sculpture look like?"

"It's a woman. Actually, it's a witch, although she looks like a normal woman because witches don't have horns or anything to differentiate them."

"Uh-huh." I stared hard into her eyes, willing her to admit the part she was so desperately trying to keep hidden.

"Fine. It was a naked woman."

I bit back a laugh as Clove's cheeks reddened and Thistle folded her arms over her chest, practically daring me to push the issue.

"Naked?" Clove sputtered. "You made a sculpture of a naked woman and put it in your new house?"

"Marcus won't let me put it in the house," Thistle countered. "He didn't like it from the start — I mean, he looked at it and then just walked away without saying a word — but then he accidentally thought it was a burglar when he got up to go to the bathroom in the middle of the night and he said it had to go."

It took everything I had not to burst out laughing. "So ... where is this sculpture now?"

Thistle narrowed her eyes to dangerous slits. "I'm not telling you. You'll steal her."

That was hardly what I had in mind. "I simply want to see her. I'm sure Marcus is overreacting. I can't take your side in an argument if I don't have a basis to form my own argument."

"Yeah, what she said," Clove echoed. "Also, we want to see the naked chick. I mean ... did you go into really fine detail? Is it like ... pornographic?"

Thistle glared so hard I was surprised laser bolts didn't shoot out of her eyes and disintegrate Clove. "It's tasteful, you ninny. I know you don't understand what that means, but I spent a lot of time on that sculpture."

"Maybe that's the problem," I suggested when my phone dinged with an incoming text. "Maybe Marcus is jealous and worried you're turning to the other side."

"What other side?"

All thoughts of continuing my verbal assault on Thistle flew out the window when I read the message. "Son of a ... ."

"What's wrong?" Clove straightened her shoulders, instantly alert. "Did Aunt Tillie do something to Mrs. Little again? I don't think I have bail money handy."

"And I'm done paying fines for her," Thistle added. "She keeps saying she'll pay us back, but she never does. I'm letting her sit in jail next time she puts a bra on that life-sized unicorn Mrs. Little bought for the front of her store. I thought the cone bra actually made that stupid fiberglass statue more interesting, but after the first two warnings Aunt Tillie should have taken the hint."

"That's not it." I sucked in a breath as I looked around my office. I'd spent three days organizing and now I couldn't remember where I'd put anything. "I need a notebook ... and pen."

My demeanor must have finally seeped into Thistle's subconscious because she turned serious. "What is going on? Did something happen?"

I nodded as I grabbed a notebook from the bin on top of the filing cabinet. My mind was careening. "There's been a plane crash on the west side of town. I mean ... an actual plane crash. It went down in Potter's Field."

"That's not far from our property," Clove said, all traces of mirth gone. "That's only a few miles from The Overlook."

"I know." I hadn't considered the proximity of the crash site to the inn. I was having too much trouble wrapping my head around the stark reality I was about to face. "I have to get out there. This is my first really big story as newspaper owner."

"We all have to get out there," Thistle said. "It's close to home and ... well, maybe we can help."

"I think a plane crash is beyond our help," Clove argued.

"You never know."

I tended to agree with Clove, but Thistle was right. There might be something we could do. "Let's get going. I need to get out there right now."

"I'll drive," Thistle offered. "We can park on the dirt road at the back of the field. That will give us easier access."

"Good idea. Let's go now."

ALIEN INSPIRATION

" I think I'd prefer a zombie apocalypse to an alien invasion. At least the zombies can't fly a spaceship. Wait ... can you imagine a zombie in a spaceship? I've always wanted to write a book. *Zombies in Space* it is. Look out world. Here it comes.
Aunt Tillie decides to be an author

TWO

A WITCHY DRAMA OF ADVENTURE AND EXPLORATION.

Unfortunately, Thistle took driving lessons under the tutelage of Aunt Tillie. The back road to Potter's Field was really a road in name only. It was more a two-track than anything, and access was limited to two points. One just happened to be conveniently located on our mothers' property.

At first, I thought we'd be better off parking on the highway and walking to the scene. We could see the smoke billowing from a mile away, and I figured it was a catastrophe on an epic scale. Once we parked, leaving Thistle's car close to the trees, I realized that Thistle's idea was much smarter because what looked to be state police troopers had already cordoned off the area near the highway, and there was no opportunity to approach without being noticed.

"What do you make of that?" Thistle's usual bravado was missing as she stared at the huge plume of smoke. "Do you think it's possible the fire will spread?"

I couldn't see actual flames, only smoke. "I don't know." I gripped my reporter's notebook close to my chest. "I'm sure they know what they're doing."

"Where did they come from?" Clove asked, joining us in front of the car. "How did they get here so fast?"

That was a very good question. Hemlock Cove is a tourist town — one of the main highways travels directly past our small hamlet — and the state police outpost is a good forty miles away. For the troopers to already be here must have meant they had an idea something was about to happen.

"I don't know," I said finally, shaking my head. "I'm guessing they won't let us get very close."

"We might not want to get close," Thistle said pragmatically. "What if there's gasoline or something in the field? That could be why there's so much smoke. It might not be safe."

"Yeah, well ... ." I trailed off when a hint of movement to my left caught my attention. I recognized the man standing a good thirty feet away, a set of binoculars in his hands, and pursed my lips as I debated his appearance. "Isn't that Hank?"

Thistle followed my gaze. "Yeah. He doesn't live far from here. Maybe he's the one who alerted the cops."

That didn't necessarily make sense to me. "He would've called the local cops. I don't see Chief Terry, do you?" I flicked my eyes back to the disaster scene. I couldn't make out the remnants of a plane, not a propeller or even hunks of metal. All I could see was the smoke and troopers busily working near the road to keep interested parties away. This is Hemlock Cove, where boredom is rampant, so a plane crash was certain to draw voyeurs. It already looked to be happening. At least ten vehicles had appeared on the road.

"I don't see him," Clove said finally. "That's not normal, right?"

I shook my head. "Chief Terry should have been the first called to the scene."

"Which means the state police are going to take over from the start," Thistle said. "Although ... some of those guys don't look like state boys. Where do you think they're from?"

I shrugged, uncertain. "Aviation circles? I believe aviation safety is handled by the Feds."

"So, where is Landon?"

Landon was Hemlock Cove's "official" FBI agent. "I don't know." Something about the scene — other than the obvious — made me uneasy. "Let's head over to Hank and see what he knows."

"Hank?" Clove's forehead puckered. "Hank is a kook."

She was right. Hank William Jenkins (yes, his mother purposely named him that) had a certain reputation in Hemlock Cove. He didn't visit town very often — only when he needed supplies — and wasn't a regular participant in the town's overblown festivals. "He lives on the other side of those trees." I gestured vaguely. "He's out here with no electricity and nothing to do but watch what happens in his little corner of the world. He's our best shot at getting answers."

Clove didn't look convinced. "But he's a pervert."

I fought the inclination to roll my eyes. "Aunt Tillie says he's a pervert. She wears leggings with dragons on them and then tells people to beware her burning loins. I don't think she's necessarily the best judge of character."

"Mrs. Little says he's a pervert, too," Clove persisted.

"Mrs. Little sells porcelain unicorns," Thistle pointed out. "Her opinion is suspect for that fact alone."

Clove decided to take one more shot at changing our minds. "I swear I once saw him watching me while I was swimming in the lake. I was naked at the time."

"You were naked in the lake?" Thistle arched a challenging eyebrow. "Were you alone or with someone?"

"Does that matter?"

"Actually, yes," I answered. "We won't be able to tease you properly if we don't have all the facts."

"Ugh. I hate you guys." Clove jutted out her lower lip. "No, seriously, I hate you guys. I wish I was an only witch."

"We all wish that," Thistle said. "Now, seriously, who were you with?"

"Rick Jordan," Clove replied, although her reticence was obvious. "It was a long time ago."

Thistle didn't bother to hide her mirth. "Was this before or after the hairlip incident?"

"He doesn't have a hairlip."

"No, but his wife does," Thistle argued. "I thought he started dating Shelly while we were still in school. How old were you when you went skinny dipping with him?"

"I didn't say I was skinny dipping."

"No, but you said you were swimming naked," I pointed out. "I believe the definition of skinny dipping is swimming naked, so ... spill."

"Fine." Clove was obviously unhappy with the turn in conversation. I would've liked to believe that would cause her to think twice before volunteering information of this nature in the future, but I knew her too well. "He was on a break from Shelly."

"You mean the hairlip," Thistle corrected.

"She's a perfectly nice woman," Clove argued. "She just happens to have a hormonal imbalance."

"She hung around with Lila," I argued, making a face at the mention of my high school enemy. Lila was the one person who always made me feel less than I was thanks to a nonstop wave of bullying and demoralization that lasted from elementary school until the day we graduated. "I don't have much sympathy for her because of that. I think the hairlip is payback."

"I don't understand why she doesn't shave that thing," Thistle argued. "It's like a caterpillar on her lip. Buy some lady shavers and call it a day. It will only take her two minutes to clean that thing up."

"Maybe she's too stupid to figure that out," I suggested. "That could be karma, too."

"I bet she's afraid there are bugs living in there," Thistle said sagely. "She probably doesn't want to unleash the fleas."

"You guys are awful." Clove was always first to turn judgmental. "That is a human being."

"She once tried to slip Nair in my shampoo in gym class," I reminded her. "She thought it was funny, and always did whatever Lila ordered her to do."

"Well, that was less human," Clove amended. "Still, that lip thing is terrible. She has to be depressed carrying that thing around."

Thistle snorted as she took the lead toward Hank. "Maybe that's her cardio. You don't know."

"I still maintain he's a pervert," Clove complained.

"Well, you were the one swimming naked in his lake." I could've been sympathetic, but, well, that's not the Winchester way. "Maybe he thought you were coming on to him."

"I was sixteen."

"And naked in his lake."

"Ugh. I hate you guys." Clove was a pouty mess by the time we caught up with Hank. He'd edged down the field a bit, seemingly intent on staring at the crash site. I was curious about what he could see with his binoculars.

"How's it going, Hank?"

He was dressed in army pants, which were offset with military boots and a tight black T-shirt. The rumor was that Hank wasn't poor. He didn't live in a small cabin with no electricity because he had to. He wanted to. Supposedly he was preparing for the end of the world. He had some special bunker or something, at least that's what I heard Mom and my aunts say once when we were kids. He was a prepper, which meant instead of watching pornography or *Keeping Up With the Kardashians* (they're basically the same thing), he prepared for the end of the world. He largely kept to himself and didn't try to recruit others, so no one paid him any attention.

"Hello." Hank's reaction was cool as he looked me up and down. "Do I know you?"

We'd met at least fifteen times over the years. He always tended to greet me the exact same way. It was his thing. "Bay Winchester," I reminded him. "I'm a reporter for The Whistler."

"Owner," Thistle automatically corrected. "You're the owner now."

Oh, right. I kept forgetting. "Owner," I said hurriedly. "I bought the newspaper a few weeks ago. I'm the owner now."

Hank blinked several times and then shook his head. "When the end of the world comes, newspapers will be obsolete. Nobody will care about the news because there will be too few people to spread it."

"You're a real ray of sunshine, aren't you?" Thistle muttered. "You just spread sunshine and flowers wherever you go."

Hank's expression didn't change when he shifted it to Thistle. "There won't be pink hair dye either."

"Well, that's one apocalypse I don't want to survive," Thistle drawled. "Who wants to live in a world without pink hair dye?"

Hank apparently wasn't much for sarcasm because he merely shrugged. "The first rule of survival is necessities. You worry about water, food and shelter — in that order — and then you worry about other things. I've never heard of anyone adding pink hair dye to a survival list."

"That's because you don't live in the Winchester world," I said brightly, hoping Hank would lose interest in arguing with Thistle and focus on me. "Pink hair dye is a must."

Hank made a derisive sound. "Tillie didn't teach you better than that? I think I need to have a talk with her."

The conversational shift threw me for a loop. "Do you talk to Aunt Tillie?"

"I don't talk to anyone if I can help it. Tillie talks to me."

Right. That made sense. Hank lived in the woods not far from our property. Aunt Tillie had a magically-cloaked pot field hidden in the hills. She also liked to hang in the woods doing ... well, I wasn't sure what she did out here. She often brought a whistle and a big stick, though for what I don't know. Whatever it was, I was convinced it wasn't good.

"Aunt Tillie does like to talk," I agreed. "What do you know about this?"

Hank's expression was blank. "About what?"

"This," I repeated.

"What?"

Thistle lost her cool. "The big ball of smoke over yonder." She waved so there could be no confusion. "What do you think that is?"

"Oh. It's a fire."

I chewed my bottom lip as I studied Hank. He was in his fifties — which put him around the same age as our mothers — and he was relatively put together for a guy who lived alone out in the middle of nowhere. While I wasn't sure he had running water, he didn't smell or anything ... and I considered that a bonus.

"Yes, but why is it on fire?" Thistle pressed. She wasn't about to back down. She didn't care if Hank was crazy, perverted or merely difficult. She liked to win, and she wasn't about to let a guy who built a hidden bunker to survive a zombie apocalypse be the one to take her down.

"Something crashed," Hank said.

"A plane?" I found my voice. "I heard it was a plane. George Thompson texted me the tip. He was making a delivery and saw the aftermath. He said whatever it was crashed into a big ball of flames."

"I think that's obviously true," Thistle said dryly. "We see the big ball of flame right over there."

"Yes, but we don't see the plane," I shot back. "There aren't any plane parts. There's no propeller or those flap things."

"That's because it wasn't a plane." Hank's tone was ominous as he lifted his binoculars. "It most definitely wasn't a plane."

Well, that was interesting. "If it wasn't a plane, what was it?"

"Flat. Disc-like. It twirled."

I wasn't sure what to make of his stilted response. "Was it some sort of drone or something?"

"I don't think they make drones big enough to cause that much damage," Clove argued. "I mean ... that's a big fire."

She had a point. Still ... . "I wasn't talking about those little drones that people can buy at Target. I was talking about the big ones the government sends on bombing missions. Maybe they were testing one here and lost control."

Thistle, never one to pass up a conspiracy theory, brightened considerably. "Oh, that's a good idea. How else did the state police get here so fast?"

"I called them," Hank replied simply.

"You called them?" My question was pointed. "Why would you call the state police directly instead of Chief Terry?"

"Terry Davenport is one of them."

"One of who?"

"You know ... one of *them*." Hank was firm. "I can't share information with one of them. It's simply not allowed."

Oh, well, I was officially lost. "Okay." I shared a quick look with Thistle, but we had to look away to keep from laughing. "So, do you think it was a drone that crashed?" I asked Hank, returning to the topic at hand.

"It wasn't a drone." Hank rolled his eyes before lifting his binoculars again. "It was a flying saucer."

I almost choked on my tongue. "Excuse me?"

"You heard what I said." Hank didn't back down. "It was a flying saucer."

"Like a UFO?" Thistle challenged.

"No. A UFO is an unidentifiable flying object. I identified this object. I was watching it before the crash. It was definitely a flying saucer."

"Huh." My stomach gave a little lurch. "How long were you watching it, Hank?"

"Oh, a good hour." Hank either didn't pick up on my worry or opted to ignore it. I didn't know him well enough to decide either way. "I've been watching it for days now. It keeps returning to this spot."

"Why do you think that is?" Clove asked, her eyes wide enough to make me wonder if she was falling for this load of crap.

"I think that there's something the aliens want." Hank was solemn. "They wouldn't keep coming back to this area if they didn't want something specific."

"And do you know what that is?" I queried.

"I do." Thistle's hand shot into the air. "They're here for Aunt Tillie. They left her here years ago and now they want to take her back. The great experiment is over. Her infiltration of the human world has been an unmitigated disaster. The aliens are calling an end to this failure of an experiment."

I scorched her with a look. "Don't encourage this insanity."

Thistle was blasé. "It makes perfect sense to me."

"It would." I blew out a sigh and shook my head. "Are you sure it wasn't some sort of small plane, Hank? I know a lot of people build airplanes with those kits now. Maybe someone built something that looked slightly different. That's a possibility, right?"

I was trying to give him an out. He didn't take it.

"No. It was a flying saucer."

"Well, great." I tugged a restless hand through my hair and turned my full attention to the billowing smoke. It showed no signs of abating. To my utter surprise, I noticed several figures moving away from the scene and in our direction. Given the location of the sun, it was impossible to make out features. All I had were silhouettes to go on. "Uh-oh."

"Do you think they're coming for us?" Clove's voice turned terrified. "They're not going to lock us up for spying on a secret government drone operation, are they?"

"Of course not."

"How can you be sure?"

"I just am." I exchanged a quick look with Thistle. I was anything but sure. Still, Clove was the type to panic. I couldn't let that happen when we were about to get some answers. "Trust me. I have everything under control."

ALIEN INSPIRATION

> If we ever get invaded by aliens, I want it to be the ones from that movie *Signs*. They traveled millions of miles to invade a world filled with water when they're allergic to it. They're also stymied by the lock on the pantry. That's exactly the kind of aliens I want to hang with.
> **Marnie shows her disinterest in all things alien**

THREE

IN HEMLOCK COVE, NO ONE CAN HEAR YOU SCREAM.

Four men approached, although making out features was difficult until they were almost on top of us. I didn't recognize the two in the lead, but the two scrambling to keep up were familiar.

"It's Landon and Chief Terry," Clove said, her relief palpable. "They'll tell us what's going on."

The looks on the faces of the men leading the charge made me wary. "Maybe. Just ... let me do the talking."

Thistle snorted, disdain practically rolling off her in waves. "No way. Whenever you do the talking we end up in trouble. I'll do the talking."

That sounded like a surefire way to get arrested. It was early spring in Hemlock Cove. That meant the snow was gone but could make an unscheduled return. I love the nicer weather — we didn't get nearly enough of it in northern Lower Michigan — so there was no way I wanted to risk being locked up for an extended period of time.

"I'll do the talking," I argued. "I'm the oldest. I'm in charge."

"That stopped being the rule when we hit ten," Thistle countered. "I'm the smartest. I should do the talking."

Now I was officially offended. "You're not the smartest. I'm the smartest."

"Well, I'm the cutest," Clove interjected. "I should definitely do the talking. I'm the best when it comes to getting us out of trouble."

"I don't think those guys are going to fall for your fake tears," I challenged. "I'm doing the talking."

"You're not doing the talking." Thistle was adamant. "I'm the one who is best prepared to handle this. Let me do it."

"Hey." The leading man called out to get our attention. "What are you doing out here?" He sounded gruff and unhappy, as if he was about to lay down the law. I immediately disliked his attitude.

"You should do the talking, Thistle," I said, changing course. "He's all yours."

Instead of being dissuaded by the man's tone, Thistle squared her shoulders. "I've got this." She plastered a bright smile on her face. "Hello, good sir. Fine day today, isn't it?"

I wrinkled my nose and touched my tongue to my top lip. "That's your big plan? You're going to attack him with stupid words? That will surely snow him."

Thistle ignored me. "Isn't spring in Michigan a lovely time?"

The man stopped when he was directly in front of us, his hands moving to his hips. He didn't look happy. "This is a restricted area. You're not allowed to be here. You need to leave right now."

He was close, and the sun was no longer blocking my view, so I had a moment to look him over. He was dressed in normal street clothes — jeans, a flannel shirt, tan boots — and he looked like he should be out running errands rather than controlling a crash site.

"I'm Bay Winchester," I offered. "I'm the owner of The Whistler, the local newspaper. We're out here trying to ascertain what happened."

"Nothing happened."

"I see." I looked to Landon, who was almost even with the first man, but he didn't make eye contact. "Well, the thing is, the residents in this area have a right to know what's going on. If this is a plane crash or something, then I have a right – actually, make that a duty – to ask questions."

"Agent Gibson, I can handle this," Landon said hurriedly. "You don't have to worry about this ... situation. I told you that."

For his part, Gibson didn't look placated by Landon's words. "And I told you, Agent Michaels, that this is my scene. You have no jurisdiction over my scene."

I didn't miss the momentary flash of agitation that crowded Landon's handsome features. He shuttered it quickly and remained calm. "It's just that I know these girls. I can get them away from the scene."

Girls? That was insulting. "I believe you mean 'women,'" I corrected.

Landon didn't smile at my poor sense of timing. "Agent Gibson, there's no reason to get upset. They're simply out here because they're curious. It's not a big deal."

There was almost a pleading edge to Landon's tone, and it set my teeth on edge. He was usually the type who would jump into the middle of the fray and start fighting. That's not how he acted today.

"What's going on?" Thistle directed the question to Chief Terry, who was out of breath as he joined the other side of Agent Gibson.

"You guys need to clear out," Chief Terry ordered. He didn't look any happier with the situation than Landon. "You can't be out here."

"This is private property," Gibson barked. "Either clear off or we'll clear you off."

Had he asked nicely, I probably would've walked away with minimal grumbling. Okay, that's not true. I still would've argued. I wouldn't have enjoyed the arguing nearly as much if he wasn't a such a tool, though.

"This isn't private property," I argued. "This is town land. Hemlock Cove bought Potter's Field from Larry Potter's estate ten years ago. They got a heckuva deal because no one else wanted it."

"It's swamp land," Clove offered helpfully. "You can't plant crops on swampland."

"And Larry Potter was his real name," Thistle added, although her tone was less than conciliatory. "He didn't appreciate Hogwarts jokes in the least."

Landon pinned Thistle with a quelling look. "That is fascinating, Thistle. That little tidbit is so important to this conversation I can't tell you how happy I am that you shared it."

Thistle ignored the sarcasm. "You're welcome."

"That doesn't change the fact that it's public land," I persisted. "You can't evict us from public land."

"That's where you're wrong." Gibson's eyes fired with fury. "If you don't leave this area right now, I will take you into custody. What's happening here is a federal matter. Federal. Do you know what that means?"

I nodded. "It means that Landon is a federal agent." I pointed toward my boyfriend, who looked as if he would rather crawl into a hole than be dragged further into the conversation. "He can tell me what's going on."

"Agent Michaels is not in control of the scene," Gibson spat. "He won't be sharing information. Isn't that right, Agent Michaels?"

Landon nodded stiffly as he met my gaze. "There's a media blackout on this one, Bay. You can't be part of it."

I was gobsmacked. Very rarely could I say that. I grew up with Aunt Tillie, after all, so I was used to being taken by surprise. Landon's reaction to all of this was something out of a freaky book, though. It just happened to be a book I had no interest in reading.

"I see." I shifted my eyes to Thistle. She looked as baffled as I felt. "So, basically you're saying that you're barring us from public land. Do I have that right?"

"Spin it however you want." Gibson refused to back down. "You're to vacate the premises right now. There is no story here. There's no information to share. I believe I've seen the newspaper you claim to own; your readers will be just as happy with a recipe for jam as they will be for information on this. You seem better suited for the jam."

My mouth dropped open as temper, rich and ripe, flared in Landon's eyes.

"Hey, don't talk to her like that," Landon snapped. "She's out here doing her job. There's no reason to give her grief."

"I'm doing my job," Gibson barked back. "You should try focusing on your job rather than these women. They're not your concern."

Landon looked as if he was going to argue further, but Chief Terry offered him an almost imperceptible shake of his head. Something very odd was going on here.

"You need to go, Bay." Landon was firm as he held my gaze. "You can't be here."

I had two options. I could stay and fight, which would almost certainly result in me being arrested and Landon being miserable, or I could meekly walk away and plot against Agent Gibson from the safety of The Overlook. To no one's surprise, I opted for the latter.

"Fine. We're going." I gave Clove a shove to push her toward Thistle's car. "You don't have to tell us twice."

"I believe I had to tell you five times," Gibson shot back.

"Oh, wow, he can count to five," Thistle drawled. "Did you use your hands or feet for that?"

Gibson's eyes flashed when I risked a glance. "Don't come back here. This property is closed to everyone but official investigators. Do you understand me?"

I refused to meet Landon's gaze as we passed in front of him. "Oh, I understand. You don't have to worry about us. We're rule followers. Ask anyone."

MY TEMPER WAS ON full display by the time we hit The Overlook.

"They're hiding something out there." I paced the kitchen as my mother and aunts toiled over dinner preparations. "The initial story I heard was a plane crash, but it didn't look like a plane crash. I think it was a drone or something. There's no other explanation for why the federal government would be out there so fast."

"Well, I hope it was a drone," my mother said, her eyes on the cake she was decorating rather than my face. "Drones are unmanned, right? If it was a drone, that means no one was hurt."

Of course, she would go there. My mother was nothing if not queen of the guilt trip. "I'm not saying that I want someone to die."

"Then what are you saying?"

"That they're hiding something, and the public has the right to know."

"I think you're blowing this out of proportion, Bay," Aunt Marnie offered without bothering to look up. She was busy chopping vegetables to go with the roast. "If it was a drone like you think, there's really nothing to report. It's not as if the federal government is going to tell us what they were doing with the drone. That's not how they operate."

How was it possible that I was the only angry one here? "They're hiding something ... and that guy talked down to us. You know I don't like getting talked down to."

"I don't blame you there." Aunt Tillie sat in her recliner in the corner. She never helped with the cooking. That was probably a good thing because, unlike my mother and aunts, she did not inherit the kitchen witch gene. She was as much of a menace when it came to cooking as I was. That meant she supervised the operation rather than participated. "I think it's obvious what's going on. This Agent Gibson was sent out to cover up for it, and you know how I feel about cover-ups."

"Oh, geez." Mom pinched the bridge of her nose and stared at the ceiling as if trying to gather her patience before exploding. "I don't think we're dealing with a cover-up. Obviously, people can't simply wander around the field because there's plane debris — or drone debris, if you like — and it's not safe for people to hang around the area."

I was incredulous. "So, you just believe that story?"

Mom shrugged. "Why wouldn't I? I think the better question is, why don't you believe it?"

"Because they're lying."

"Darned right." Aunt Tillie's face flushed with excitement as she leaned forward. That was never a good sign. She was the only one on my side in this particular argument, though, so I ignored the fact that she often made me nervous when it came to things like this. "I think I know what they're lying about."

"You do?" I arched a curious eyebrow. "What were they doing out there? Have you seen a drone flying around?" Something occurred to me. "Wait, you didn't arrange for that drone to crash because it was flying over your pot field, did you? If so, that is not cool."

Mom's shoulders stiffened as she shifted to face Aunt Tillie. "You didn't crash that drone, did you?"

"Who do you take me for?" Aunt Tillie can't often pull off indignant with anyone who knows her, but she gave it a decent shot today. "I wouldn't crash a drone. It can't see my medicinal field anyway. It's cloaked."

Actually, that was a minor relief. If the Feds didn't know the pot field was there, the odds of us being the target of their little spying mission were slim. "If they weren't here for us, what were they here for?"

"You're looking at it the wrong way," Aunt Tillie chided. "It wasn't the government spying at all."

"So it was a plane?" I couldn't help feeling a bit disappointed. "Do you think someone died? Who around here has a plane like that?"

The look Aunt Tillie shot me was pitying. "It wasn't a plane either. Are you stupid?"

"Is that a rhetorical question?"

"Apparently you are stupid." She made a clucking sound with her tongue. "It was a flying saucer, Bay. Everybody knows that."

I stared at her for a long beat, blinking rapidly. Finally, I found my voice. "Are you kidding me?"

"No. It was a flying saucer. I know it and you know it, too."

"I know nothing of the sort," I snapped. "I know something went down in that field, but it most certainly wasn't a UFO."

"Of course it wasn't a UFO." Aunt Tillie's tone turned weary. "It wasn't an unidentifiable flying object. It was a flying saucer. It was identified."

Now it was my turn to be suspicious. "Have you been hanging out with Hank?"

"Of course not. He's a nut."

"You're a nut, too," Mom argued. "I warned you about hanging out with him. He supposedly has an illegal arsenal on his property ... and explosives, if you believe the gossip in town. I don't think you should be around explosives."

That was the understatement of the year. "Hank was out there. He called it a flying saucer, too."

"Well, I don't think you have to worry about it being a flying saucer," Mom said. "I think your guess that it was a drone is probably spot on. It makes the most sense. If someone around here had a plane and it didn't return to the hangar, we all would've heard about it."

"I'm still going to find out exactly what happened."

"Of course you are, dear." Mom absently brushed me aside as she moved around the counter. "Can you figure it out in the other room? We're on a bit of a timetable here."

And just like that, I was dismissed. "Fine." I moved toward the door. "Apparently I'm not appreciated anywhere."

"Don't look at me," Aunt Tillie groused. "I definitely don't appreciate you. When you agree it's a flying saucer, then we'll talk."

"You're going to be waiting a long time."

"I bet I don't wait very long at all."

I WAS ALONE IN THE library when Landon let himself into the inn for dinner. He headed straight for me, and when we locked gazes he looked angry rather than apologetic.

"I'm not in the mood to be yelled at," I warned, my temper returning with a vengeance. "I didn't do anything wrong."

Landon held his hands up. "Did I say you did something wrong?"

"Kind of. You basically gave me the bum's rush and ordered me off public property."

"I had no choice, Bay. I'm not in charge of this case. I can't give you special treatment."

Oh, that was rich. "I don't believe I asked for special treatment."

"You don't have to ask. I give it to you whenever I can because I love and trust you."

If he thought a big pile of mush would cause me to melt, he had another think coming. "I wasn't asking for special treatment today. I was on public land. Removing me from the scene was against the law."

"Then perhaps you should file a complaint." Landon flopped down on the couch next to me and pinched the bridge of his nose. "I need a drink."

I wasn't about to wait on him given what had happened in Potter's Field. "The drink cart is on the other side of the room."

He slid me a sidelong look, his expression so weary that it caused a momentary jolt of guilt to course through me. My anger quickly swallowed the guilt, though.

"Are you going to be angry with me all night?" Landon asked finally.

I shrugged, noncommittal. "I guess that depends."

"On what? If you want a massage, I'll gladly give you one when we get back to the guesthouse. I'm even tired enough for us to take a bath together and go to bed early."

That wasn't exactly what I had in mind. "I want to know what's going on in Potter's Field. I know you couldn't tell me earlier, but Agent Give Me a Migraine is nowhere in sight. He can't stop you from talking now."

Landon worked his jaw, but no sound came out. Finally, when he decided what to say, it was the last thing I wanted to hear. "I can't tell you. This is a priority case. That means I can't talk to anyone, let alone a representative of the press."

"I'm not just a representative of the press. I'm your girlfriend."

"It doesn't matter. I can't talk about this investigation. I've been specifically ordered to keep my mouth shut. Everyone involved with the investigation has been ordered to do the same. If there are any leaks there will be hell to pay."

I fought to remain stoic. "So ... you don't trust me."

"It's not that. I trust you more than anyone. I wouldn't have given you my heart otherwise. This is my job, Bay. I can't share information on this one. I'm sorry."

He rarely cut me out of investigations. In fact, he shared more freely than he should. Still, I couldn't stop myself from being agitated. I knew it wasn't his fault. That didn't stop the small ember of frustration that had been burning all afternoon in my gut from exploding into an inferno. "I see."

"Bay, please don't make this a thing. I can't take an argument right now."

He looked so miserable I acquiesced, but only on the surface. "Fine. I won't make it a thing. I won't ask again what's going on in Potter's Field."

"Thank you." Landon leaned over to offer a kiss, but I smoothly slid off the couch. "I need to check on dinner preparations. You should get yourself a drink."

Landon heaved out a weighted sigh. "You're not letting this go, are you?"

"Of course I am."

"Why don't I believe you?"

I shrugged. "I have no idea." Actually, I had a very good idea. It was because I was lying. There was no way I was going to let this go now. It was too big to ignore.

ALIEN INSPIRATION

> Do you think the aliens in *War of the Worlds* attacked because we're jerks or they simply found Tom Cruise ludicrous as an action hero? He's shorter than Aunt Tillie, for crying out loud. I think it was Cruise rage more than anything else.
> **Winnie on alien motivations**

FOUR

WE WITCHES ARE NOT ALONE.

"*H*ow long are you going to stay angry?"

Landon picked an easy pace as we left The Overlook after breakfast the next morning. I wasn't particularly interested in arguing in front of my family, but we only had oatmeal to eat in the guesthouse. Compared to the eggs and hash browns I knew my mother would be making, there was no competition.

We had stayed through dinner and dessert the previous evening before heading home. I didn't have my vehicle — I'd left it downtown when Thistle insisted on driving the day before — so I walked back to the guesthouse. Landon had no choice but to drive, but I didn't miss the whisper of irritation on his face when I opted not to go with him.

I understood my attitude was juvenile and ridiculous. I wasn't naive enough to believe otherwise. That didn't mean his refusal to at least give me a hint on where to start looking didn't sting.

For the first time since we'd moved in together, we weren't on the best of terms when sleep beckoned. He slept on his side of the bed, I stayed on mine, and I woke up crabbier than when I went to sleep. That agitation carried over through breakfast, which my mother and aunts wisely decided to ignore.

"I don't know how long I'm going to stay angry," I admitted as we walked the pathway back to the guesthouse. "I've never been in this position before with you, so I don't have a baseline to work with."

"And what position is that?"

"The one where you shut me out."

Landon made an angry sound, like a wounded cat, in the back of his throat. "I am not shutting you out. You're shutting me out."

"That is a ridiculous claim."

"That doesn't mean it's untrue."

I slowed my pace and opened my mouth, ready to argue to the point harsh words would most definitely be said, but I caught myself. Neither of us liked to fight. Er, well, at least we didn't like big fights. Little ones were okay because they served as a foreplay of sorts, but big fights left us both feeling off.

Rather than engage my immature instincts, I sucked in a steadying breath. "I don't want this to blow up."

Landon's usually expressive eyes were unreadable as they scanned me. "I don't want it to blow up either, but I can't give you information. I've been ordered not to. I have a job to do."

"You've gone against orders before," I reminded him. "I believe you went against orders the night we met. You weren't supposed to go out of your way to worry about me that night because it put your entire undercover operation at risk. You showed up anyway."

"That was different. I knew you were in real trouble. What I didn't know at the time was that you were magical and could probably take care of yourself. Even knowing that, I still would've come."

"So why is this situation different?"

"You know why."

I honestly didn't. "Not really."

"Bay, you were in danger of dying that night," Landon snapped. "I thought you were in real trouble, and even though I didn't know you that well I didn't want to risk something happening to you. I couldn't live with it even then. You're not in danger here."

"I'm in danger of losing my mind if you don't tell me what crashed in that field."

Instead of reacting out of frustration, Landon smiled. "This right here, this natural curiosity you can't seem to rein in, this is the thing you got from Aunt Tillie."

If he was trying to make up, he picked a rotten way to do it. "I am not like Aunt Tillie."

"Oh, but you are." He refused to back down. "You all are. None of you are exactly like her — which is a blessing — but you all have a little something from her. Thistle got the biggest dose, but you come in a close second. You think just like her sometimes, and now is an example of that."

I worked my jaw as I glared at him. Finally, I could think of only one thing to say. "That's the meanest thing you've ever said to me."

Landon snickered as he smoothed my hair and pressed a kiss to my forehead. He was used to having a few minutes of quiet time to talk before we got up every morning. That didn't happen today, and I was starting to believe that it unsettled both of us – which only furthered my mother's argument that we were co-dependent.

"I didn't say it was a bad thing that you had a streak of Aunt Tillie in you," he pointed out. "For the record, it's not bad. It is, however, annoying when I can't give you what you want. We all have orders to follow."

I wanted to push him. I wanted to wheedle and get my own way. That wasn't fair to him, though. We were both trying to grow a bit since we'd taken the huge step of sharing a roof. That growth spurt wasn't always seamless, but it was working fairly well.

"I don't want you to tell me." I held my hands up in defeat. "It's not fair to ask for information you've been ordered not to tell."

"I would tell you if I could. You know that."

"I do." I bobbed my head in confirmation. "It's just hard because you usually share information, even when you're not supposed to. We're often a team on stuff like this."

Landon's eyes narrowed as he extended a finger. "Don't do that. You know I don't like it when you do that."

I adopted an air of innocence. "Do what?"

"That." Landon's forehead wrinkled as he slid a strand of black hair behind his ear. "We are a team. You know that. You've helped me so many ways I've lost count. I like to think I've helped you, too."

"You have."

"Those other times were different," Landon persisted. "We were always working to solve a case that put others at risk. You know, find a murderer and whatnot. No one is at risk here."

"You don't know that. What if that drone is leaking some airborne poison or something? That could hurt people."

Landon planted his hands on his hips. "Do you really think I would keep you in the dark if poison was leaking into the ecosystem?"

He had a point. I couldn't back down now, though. "You didn't deny it was a drone."

"I can't confirm or deny anything."

I stared hard into his eyes, willing him to break. He merely stared back.

"Fine." My frustration threatened to bubble over into whining, so I had no choice but to give in if I didn't want to argue. Things were going well between us now and we hadn't really clashed in weeks. I didn't want to break the streak. Oh, sure, I knew it would eventually happen because we were fiery people, but I wasn't in the mood to push it now. "You have to keep things secret. I get it."

"Do you?" Landon cupped my chin and tilted my head up. Instead of worry flitting through his eyes I found amusement. "Do you want to know what I think?"

"Not particularly."

"I think you're going to keep pursuing this no matter what. You're not the type who can let it go."

"I can let things go."

"Not this. You took it as a personal affront when Gibson made you leave the scene yesterday. You don't like being told what to do."

"No one likes being told what to do."

"Fair enough." Landon surprised me when he planted a quick kiss on my lips before pulling me into a hug. "You're going to do what you're going to have to do, and I'll do what I have to do. I get that."

Wait ... what was he saying? "You're not going to try to keep me from investigating this?" I was leery. I couldn't help it.

"If I thought it would work, I would definitely try," Landon replied. "But it won't. We both know that. You can't stop yourself. Besides that, I don't want to change you. I like how diligent you are."

"Diligent makes me sound boring."

Landon chuckled. "You're never boring."

"It's just ... this is the biggest story that has crossed my desk since I bought the newspaper. I can't let it go."

Landon's expression softened. "I know. But you need to be careful."

"Because someone is out in the woods hoping to steal government drone secrets?"

Encouraging me was most definitely the last thing on his mind, but Landon smiled all the same. "Because Agent Gibson has a stick up his butt — something I never thought I would say about a superior until I spent so much time with Winchester witches. And he won't hesitate to arrest you if he catches you snooping around. You need to be careful."

"Chief Terry won't arrest me." I was almost certain of that. "You won't either."

"Not by choice," Landon cautioned. "You know I can't handle the guilt associated with arresting you."

I knew it hurt him more than me. "I'll be careful."

"Make sure that you do," Landon pressed. "He can have you taken to a federal facility. He has the authority to do that. I need you to be really careful when you're sneaking around. In fact, if you know a spell to make yourself invisible ... or to make you look like someone else ... that would be great. You need to hide what you're doing from the Feds, who will be all over Hemlock Cove the next few days."

That was interesting. He'd let something slip and didn't realize it. "You're a Fed," I said finally. "Do I have to hide what I'm doing from you?"

"There are different levels of Feds. As for me, I always want to know that you're safe. We'll play the rest of it by ear. If you get in trouble, I want to know about it. Nothing changes that."

I nodded, my mind busy. "Okay. I can work around that."

"You have no idea the fear you just sent coursing up my spine." Landon pressed my body tightly against his. "I don't want to fight about this, Bay. I have a job to do. I understand you have a job to do, too. Just ... be careful."

I relaxed against him long enough to rest my head against his shoulder. "I'll be careful."

"Good." He kissed my forehead. "Try to keep Aunt Tillie in line, too."

Surprised, I leaned back. "Aunt Tillie? I'm not bringing her with me."

"Oh, she'll end up with you." Landon looked resigned. "She won't be able to stay away. Don't let her carry that shotgun into the woods for the next few days. It's going to be crawling with agents, and they won't find it funny if she runs her usual shtick on them."

Hmm. He let another something slip. Instead of pointing it out, I patted his back. "We'll be good."

Landon cocked a dubious eyebrow. "You won't be good."

"We'll be careful," I corrected.

"That's the most I can ask for." Landon took me by surprise and caused me to giggle when he dipped me low and gave me a lavish kiss. "Remember, if you get arrested I won't be able to do that until we find a way to get you out of jail. It might take days to make that happen."

"You'll get me out of jail no matter what, though, right?"

"Yeah." Landon's expression softened. "No matter what."

"That's all I need to hear." I put a hand to either side of his face. "It'll be fine. In fact, it'll be a blast from the past. It will be like when we first met and were forced to tiptoe around each other."

"I know you might find this hard to believe, but I didn't particularly enjoy that part of our relationship."

"I did. Whenever I saw you, I got butterflies in my stomach. It was ... invigorating."

Landon's smile widened. "I think that might be the nicest thing you've ever said to me."

"I love you," I supplied. "That's nice, too."

"Even nicer." Landon smacked a loud kiss on my lips. "I love you, too. Don't get arrested."

"I won't." I hoped that was true. "I need a ride into town. I left my car at Hypnotic."

"You've got it. I'm starting at the police station today. It works out well."

AGENT GIBSON STOOD outside the police station when Landon parked. Clove and Thistle's shop, Hypnotic, was across the street, so I didn't have far to walk. The look on Gibson's face when he saw Landon and me together was enough to make me cringe.

"Did he not know we were a couple?"

Landon looked grim as he stood next to his Explorer and frowned. "He knew. I told him after you left. He told me my personal life was none of his concern, but he would have no problem locking you up if it came to that. That's why I was so adamant you leave. Luckily for us, Mrs. Little showed up a few minutes after and he found her more annoying than you."

"That was lucky."

Landon smirked as he moved my hair away from my face. "Be good. Don't get into too much trouble. Do not let Aunt Tillie call the shots when you add her to your team."

I had no idea where he was getting that. There was no way I would purposely add Aunt Tillie to my team. "She's not joining the party."

"She always joins the party." Landon moved to give me a kiss, but the way Gibson glowered caused him to take a step back. He looked annoyed more than amused by the man's weighted glare. "If I'm around at lunch and can get away I'll bring you something at the newspaper office."

"I probably won't be there."

"I know. But you gave me a key, and I might need to hide."

"There's a couch if you need to take a nap."

"Naps aren't nearly as much fun if you're not there to take one with me."

"Sweet."

"I'm just killing time because I don't want to talk to that man." Landon inclined his chin in Gibson's direction. "He's not exactly what I would call fun."

"Well, you'll survive." I patted his arm and started to move across the street. "I'll see you later. I'll text you if I'm going to be late getting back to the inn."

"You do that." Landon waved as Gibson moved to stand next to him. The man's voice carried, so I had no trouble hearing his first volley of the morning.

"She's jaywalking."

"There's no one driving down the street," Landon shot back. "Her cousins' store is right there, and traffic is non-existent. Why is this an issue?"

"The law is the law."

I ignored the ridiculous argument and turned my attention to the woman shuffling along the sidewalk in front of Hypnotic. I recognized her right away, although she was hardly what I would consider a family friend.

"Hello, Mrs. Little."

Margaret Little was something of a family inconvenience. Heck, she was a pain in the keister for the entire town. She'd fought with Aunt Tillie for decades and considered herself in charge of Hemlock Cove. Still, she was a magnet for good gossip sometimes and if she was at the scene of the crash yesterday she might have information.

Instead of greeting me with a sneer or snort, Mrs. Little blandly stared past me. Was she playing a game? Was this her version of ignoring me?

"Mrs. Little, did you hear me?"

Mrs. Little slowly turned to face me, as if some outside power was forcing her to react. When she finally focused, there didn't seem to be much recognition behind her eyes. "I heard you." Her voice sounded jumpy. "There's no reason to yell."

"I wasn't yelling."

"I think I know yelling when I hear it." That snippy outburst sounded more like the Mrs. Little I knew and loathed.

"I just wanted to ask if you saw anything while you were out at the scene yesterday," I said. "I couldn't get close enough to see anything, but I'm hoping to track down information today."

"'The scene?'" Mrs. Little furrowed her brow. "What 'scene' are you talking about?"

My heart skipped a beat. "The scene of the crash in the woods. Are you saying you don't remember that happening?" My mind was busy with possibilities. Mrs. Little looked lost, making me wonder if perhaps she'd had a stroke or some sort of spell (and not the witchy kind). I put my hand on her arm. "Are you feeling okay?"

"I'm feeling fine, Clove!" Mrs. Little's eyes filled with fire. "Don't worry about me. Mind your own business. Of course, I remember what happened in the woods yesterday. I'm not an idiot."

"No one said you were an idiot. Although ... you did just call me Clove."

"Of course, I did. That's your name."

I swallowed hard. "My name is Bay."

"That's what I said!" Mrs. Little looked close to exploding. "Why are you even out here bothering me, Bay?"

I held my hands up in capitulation. "I'm sorry to have bothered you." I took a step back, unsure what to do. However I tackled the situation, it was best not to push Mrs. Little in case she was having some sort of medical episode. I would have to call one of her friends to check on her. I saw no other option. "Take it easy, Mrs. Little."

"I'll do what I want when I want," Mrs. Little fired back. "I'm certainly not going to listen to the likes of you."

I'd already figured that out. "Have a nice day."

She didn't respond. I didn't expect her to. Seriously, though, she was acting even weirder than normal. Something was up.

ALIEN INSPIRATION

> I've given it a lot of thought. Take *Invasion of the Body Snatchers*, for example. I think people were reading that situation wrong. Imagine how much better it would be if I took everyone over and directed them how to act. That's a genius idea. The world would be a better place.
> **Aunt Tillie plotting against the world**

FIVE

CONSUME MASS QUANTITIES ... OF BACON!

I told Thistle and Clove about my run-in with Mrs. Little, but they weren't exactly worked up about the development.

"Maybe she's finally giving in to her inner crazy person," Thistle suggested as she bagged herbs for the store's display shelves. "We've always known the crazy was in there. It might be nice, maybe more comfortable, if she finally let it out to play."

"She didn't seem normal," I argued. "She was almost sleepwalking. I think something might actually be wrong with her. I was thinking about calling Nora Dombrowski to check on her. She's a retired registered nurse. I figure it couldn't do any harm."

Thistle shrugged. "Go ahead, but I think you're wasting your time."

"You didn't see her." I couldn't let it go. "There's no way you would believe she was acting normal if you'd seen her."

"Then call." Thistle focused on her work. "You don't have anything better to do, right? It's not as if you can go out to the scene and look around."

"Oh, I'm going back to the scene."

Clove, who was working behind the counter, jerked her head in my direction. "You'll get arrested if you go back out there. You heard that Gibson guy. He'll take you into custody."

"I'm not worried about that. I have a plan."

Thistle and Clove groaned in unison.

"Oh, don't say things like that," Thistle complained. "You sound like Aunt Tillie."

"You take that back."

"No. It's true."

"I am nothing like that woman."

"You can say it all you want. I know you're exactly like her."

She was clearly trying to pick a fight. I didn't have time for that. "I'm going back out there. I'm simply not going to approach from where they would expect."

"Where are you going to approach from?"

"Hollow Creek."

Instead of explaining the myriad ways she thought my plan was stupid, Thistle merely cocked her head. "That's not a bad idea. They won't see you park there, and because they're outsiders they won't know about the shallow part where you can walk straight across. They probably won't be watching the area. That's smart."

I preened. "I thought so."

"They'll still arrest you if they find you."

My smile slipped. "They won't find me. I'm smarter than them."

Thistle snorted. "If you say so." She closed a bag of herbs. "I'd volunteer to go with you, but ... well, I don't want to. I'm not nearly as interested in this as you are."

"I'm fine with that. I'll have a better chance of slipping under the radar alone."

"Just be careful," Clove cautioned. "If you get arrested, I don't think you'll be able to bail your way out with kisses. Only Landon would allow that, and he's clearly not in charge."

"Landon knows I'm going to keep pursuing this. He's fine with it."

"Is that what he said or what you heard?" Thistle challenged.

"It's what he said ... kind of."

"That's what I thought. You'd better be careful. I don't think Agent Gibson is messing around."

"Neither am I." I zipped the front of my hoodie. "That's why I have to get going. Clove, I need you to call Nora and tell her to check on Mrs. Little. Do you think you can do that?"

Clove balked. "Why does it have to be me?"

"Because I said so. I'm the oldest and what I say goes."

"Whatever." Clove rolled her eyes. "I'll call, but only because I'm a little concerned, too. Maybe we'll get lucky and they'll lock Mrs. Little up because she really is crazy."

"I would prefer her being crazy than something else," I admitted. "I have to get going. I'll be in touch."

"And we'll be waiting for updates with bated breath," Thistle teased. "Have fun with the government conspiracy."

"You joke, but I plan to break this wide open. Just you wait."

I WAS FAMILIAR WITH Hollow Creek, so I knew exactly where to park to obscure my car. The creek was running faster than normal because it was spring. We'd had a lot of snow during the winter, which meant the creek ran higher than normal. Still, I rolled up my pants and took off my shoes, carrying a towel to the other side so I could dry off my feet and climb back into my sneakers before setting off through the woods toward Potter's Field. I left the towel behind for my return trip. The water was cold enough that my toes felt numb, but I sent a bit of warming magic through my socks and I barely noticed as I cut through the trees.

It was a mile-long hike. The distance didn't bother me as much as the isolation. I grew up in the woods, playing with my cousins in the trees whenever the mood struck. I wasn't afraid of the trees, but I wasn't keen on making the hike alone. I didn't have an option, though, so I sucked it up.

The closer I got to the scene, the more noises I heard. Most of the noise came in the form of people talking to each other, but I could also make out heavy equipment — perhaps a tractor — as rescue crews toiled in the field. I slowed my pace and stuck to the trees so I could watch, pulling up short when I caught the first hint of movement.

Potter's Field bustled with activity. There had to be at least forty people working in the field, and most of them appeared to be wearing some sort of protective gear. They looked kind of like blue space suits. The suits boasted helmets of sorts with what looked to be Plexiglas covering the faces. The workers walked in tandem, about five feet apart, and searched the field in a grid pattern. I recognized it from forest searches for missing children, a few of which I'd been a part of over the years, so I understood what was happening.

They were searching for something. But what?

I squinted as I stared at the field. There was no longer any smoke rising, but a heavy cloud remained over the area, and the scent that lingered was almost overwhelming. I enjoyed a good bonfire as much as anyone, so smoke didn't usually bother me. This was something else entirely. Along with the smoky scent, I could just make out a more acrid smell.

My biggest problem was the fact that I couldn't make out the lines of an aircraft in the blackened part of the field. Clearly, a fire had burned long and hot, but the remnants of the drone (or plane, if they were sticking to the original story) should still be visible. There was nothing.

I stared for a long time, practically willing myself to find something to see. I reasoned that it was there but somehow obscured, perhaps hiding in plain sight like one of those posters in which you have to relax your eyes to see the hidden picture. There was always the possibility that the craft hit so hard it plowed into the ground and broke into a thousand bits on contact. That seemed unlikely, but it was all I had to work with.

I was lost in thought as I watched the work, stirring only when a cry went out amongst the searchers and I jerked my head to the left. At first, I didn't understand what was happening. One of the men in the search grid was on his knees and several other workers converged on him, concern evident. My initial thought was that he'd found whatever they were looking for.

Then something else happened.

A man in a silver suit that was much like the others, but fancier, shoved the other searchers out of the way as he approached the man on the ground. It was hard to hear, but I listened hard and picked up a few stray bits of conversation.

"... burns on his hands ... ."

"Looks to have spread to his chest."

"... having trouble breathing and ... look at that."

I wanted to run over and get a better look but remained hidden from sight. I cursed myself for not lifting Aunt Tillie's binoculars before leaving the inn this morning. I didn't even think about it, but I was so far away I couldn't make out anything. If I detached from the trees now, made my presence known, I would surely be taken into custody.

No matter how my curiosity spiked, I was stuck in the trees with no way to ascertain what was really happening.

I watched for what felt like a long time. Eventually, the fallen man was taken from the field and transported to what looked to be a medical van on the far side of the field. It was white with red marks on the side. Even though I tried to zoom in with my phone, I couldn't make out the lettering on the side of the van. I was simply too far away.

Not long after the man was dragged away, the search resumed. I stayed hidden in my spot for at least an hour, but no one called out again. Apparently, they found nothing else. But the search continued.

What the heck was going on out here?

I HAD MORE QUESTIONS than answers by the time I returned to town. I parked in front of Hypnotic, intending to slip inside so I could describe what I'd seen to Thistle and Clove and hash things out. Instead, when I saw Landon's Explorer in front of the diner, I headed in that direction.

Even though I knew he was incapable of answering my questions, I couldn't stop myself.

Chief Terry and Landon sat at their usual table — no sign of Agent Gibson — when I entered. Landon immediately lifted his head, as if he sensed me, and smiled as I approached.

"Hey, sweetie." He stood and pulled out a chair for me. "I wasn't sure you were around this afternoon. I went to the newspaper office, but you weren't there."

"Did you go inside?"

Landon nodded. "I did. You've been working hard. You definitely need to get some art in there. I don't like the blank walls."

"You sound like Thistle."

"I won't fight with you despite the fact that you said that." Landon returned to his chair, his eyes keen as they roamed my face. "You look tired. Where have you been?"

I shrugged as I slid out of my hoodie. "Out and about. Nowhere special."

Landon clearly didn't believe me because he narrowed his eyes. "Why are you lying?"

His tone grated. "I thought we talked about this after breakfast. We both have jobs to do, right? This time our jobs simply can't coexist, so we're not sharing information."

"I don't remember specifically agreeing to that."

"Yeah, well, that's how things turned out." I plucked a menu from the center of the table and opened it. "Oh, they have hot beef sandwiches on special. That sounds good."

"Comfort food," Chief Terry agreed, speaking for the first time. "You look tired, Bay. Didn't you sleep last night?" The look he shot Landon was accusatory. "Didn't you let her sleep last night?"

"Oh, geez." Landon rolled his eyes. "Don't turn this into something it isn't. Bay was upset with me last night because of what happened with Gibson. We didn't exactly fight, although we didn't exactly get along either. She slept. It wasn't some long and overblown affair or anything."

"He's right. I slept." I flashed a smile for Chief Terry's benefit. I had a father of my own. He hadn't lived in Hemlock Cove for half of my life, but he'd moved back about a year ago. I considered Chief Terry my second father. We were unbelievably tight. "I've just been busy."

"Doing what?" Chief Terry knew me well, so he was instantly suspicious.

"Well, for starters, have you seen Mrs. Little today?" I thought distracting Landon and Chief Terry was probably my best option.

Landon furrowed his brow. "Why would I want to see Mrs. Little? She's generally the last person on my wish list when it comes to friendly town interaction."

"I didn't seek her out. Trust me. I ran into her when I was going to Hypnotic."

"I haven't seen her since yesterday," Chief Terry supplied. "She was all fired up about what was going on in Potter's Field, demanding answers even though she has no standing to demand anything. I mean ... she's head of the Downtown Development Authority, for crying out loud. It's not as if she's the mayor."

"Do you guys even have a mayor?" Landon moved his hand to the back of my neck and idly rubbed. It was as if he could sense the tension pooling there. "I don't think I've ever met the mayor."

"We have a mayor." Chief Terry's expression darkened. "He doesn't really do anything, though. He's more of a figurehead."

"The council runs the town," I explained. "The mayor barely shows up for the council meetings."

"Oh, right. I think you've told me that before." Landon dug into my tense muscles. "Why are you so tense?"

I thought about what I'd seen in Potter's Field and shrugged. "It's been a long morning. It started with running into Mrs. Little. She was acting off."

Chief Terry snorted. "As compared to what? That woman has been off since the day I met her. I was a kid and she was an adult when that happened, so that's saying something."

"No, not 'off' like mean and nasty, like she usually is," I argued. "It was more like she wasn't entirely there. She didn't see me at first, which is difficult to understand because she was practically on top of me. I had to speak to her twice before she responded."

Chief Terry sobered. "You're really worried about her, aren't you?"

"I am." I nodded. "She seemed confused. I was trying to get information from her in case she saw something at Potter's Field yesterday — don't give me grief about that, by the way, because I'm not in the mood — but she seemed confused about what I was asking. Then she referred to me as Clove."

Landon leaned closer. "She called you Clove?"

"Yeah. She was out of it. Her eyes were glazed, and I was worried. I tried to talk to her, to offer help, but then she snapped back to her usual terrible self and it was as if I'd imagined everything ... although I know I didn't imagine anything."

Landon and Chief Terry exchanged confused looks.

"What do you think it was?" Chief Terry asked, legitimately curious.

I shrugged. "I don't know. I was jarred enough by the exchange that I asked Clove to call Nora Dombrowski to check on her. I figured that Nora would better recognize the signs of a stroke or something and because they're friends Mrs. Little would be less likely to pitch a fit."

"That was smart," Chief Terry said. "What did Nora say?"

"I didn't talk to her. I had someplace else to be. Clove did it for me. I haven't checked back in with Clove yet."

"Well, I'll take the time to check on her after lunch," Chief Terry offered. "You know, just to be on the safe side."

"That's good. Thank you." When I shifted my gaze to Landon, I found him staring at me with unveiled interest. "What?"

"You said you had someplace else to be. Where was that?"

My antenna went up and I purposely kept my face blank. "Just some work stuff."

"What work stuff?"

Well, if he wanted to push, I could turn the tables and do the same. "What did you guys do this morning?"

"We worked with Agent Gibson," Landon replied without hesitation. "You know that. You also know we can't talk about that."

"Well, I can't talk about my work either," I said primly. "We both agreed that we would keep to our official sides of the line on this one. I had things to do this morning. So did you. It is what it is."

Landon scowled. "I hate this. Just ... tell me what you were doing. It'll drive me crazy if you don't."

For the first time since I realized he wouldn't be sharing information I found myself enjoying the situation. If I was driving him crazy, at least we were on even footing. "I can't tell you. I mean ... I could ... but then I'd have to kill you. It's top secret. I'm simply following orders."

"Oh, good grief." Landon shot Chief Terry an incredulous look. "Can you believe she's playing things this way?"

"I think it sounds exactly right." Chief Terry chuckled, amused. "She'll only get worse the longer this carries on. She said it herself. It is what it is. We can't change it. She can't change it either."

"That doesn't mean I have to like it," Landon shot back. "She'll drive me insane running all over the place without telling me where she's going. It's not funny!"

Chief Terry's shoulders shook with silent laughter. "It's a little funny."

"It won't be funny if she runs afoul of Gibson and gets arrested."

In an instant, Chief Terry sobered. "You're right. That won't be funny. Bay, you'd better watch yourself."

Even though I'd felt exhausted only minutes before, I brightened considerably. Things were looking up. Eventually, Landon would have no choice but to crack and tell me what was going on because he wouldn't be able to take my secrecy. All I had to do was wait him out.

"You don't have to worry about me." I smiled and waved at the waitress so she knew I was ready to place my order. "I have everything under control. Trust me."

"Ugh. This is going to suck," Landon muttered. "You're already channeling Aunt Tillie."

"Yes, well, you said it yourself. Sometimes she's helpful in situations like this."

"I hate being right."

I patted his leg under the table. "You'll live. However, if you can't tell me about your day — and vice versa — we have absolutely nothing to discuss. We'll have to cover alternative subjects."

Landon cocked an eyebrow. "Alternative subjects?"

"Yes. For example, how do you feel about the latest global warming reports?"

Landon's mouth dropped open. "Are you trying to torture me?"

That was only a side benefit. He simply didn't realize it yet.

ALIEN INSPIRATION

> Live long and prosper. Wait, that's not what I want. Live long and shut your hole. Yup, that's better.
>
> **Thistle designing her own form of the Vulcan blessing**

SIX

IT IS EVERYTHING YOU DREAM OF. IT IS NOTHING YOU CAN CURSE.

*L*unch turned out to be more fun than I'd envisioned. Chief Terry noticed the dirt on my shoes as we were leaving the diner, which caused Landon to bend down and study them. He was an investigator, after all. He couldn't take not knowing all the facts.

I was appropriately evasive when answering, explaining that I loved spring because it meant I could finally enjoy the great outdoors. I left Landon with a kiss and a smile before heading to Hypnotic. I made a big show of stopping in the doorway to wave before entering.

Thistle and Clove looked up from their sandwiches, amusement lighting their features as I threw myself on the couch next to Thistle.

"You look like you're in a good mood," Thistle commented. "How did your trip to ground zero go?"

My smile slipped a bit as I remembered my trip to Potter's Field. "Not great. I couldn't get close." I explained what I'd seen, leaving nothing out, and finished with a retelling of my lunch with Landon and Chief Terry. "Landon isn't having as much fun as he was yesterday when keeping me in the dark. He doesn't like the tables being turned."

"I don't blame him," Clove said. "You're approaching it in a smart way. He'll probably crumble and tell you something before all is said and done."

"That's what I'm hoping for."

"What about the guy you saw carried away?" Thistle asked. "You said it sounded as though he had burned hands. How does that happen in the middle of a field?"

"I have no idea." I was completely sober now. "It was creepy. They were all wearing those spaceship-suits you see in movies. I swear I saw at least eight episodes of *The X-Files* where people were wearing those suits, and none of them ended well."

"Oh, well, if you saw it on *The X-Files*, it must be true," Thistle shook her head. "Seriously, that doesn't sound normal."

"No, and I smelled something out there. I'm not sure what it was — it's hard to describe, kind of like ammonia only stronger, and mixed with some witch hazel to really make your eyes water. It was definitely more than smoke."

"It sounds like you had an easy time walking across Hollow Creek to approach," Thistle noted. "That's good to know in case you want to go back."

"Yeah, definitely. What about Mrs. Little, Clove? Did you call Nora?"

Clove nodded as she swallowed. "I did. I explained everything you told me. Nora said it was probably nothing — Mrs. Little does hate you and would take great joy in unnerving you — but she promised to check on her."

"At least that's something." I leaned back on the couch and rested my hands on my thighs. "Chief Terry said he would check on her, too. Landon didn't seem to care that she was acting odd, but he had other things on his mind."

"Do you think he knows that you went back to the scene?" Clove asked. "He can't be happy if he suspects that."

"He knows me well enough to know that I have no choice but to check out the field. He's not happy, but we're in a position we've never been in before. Usually, he's the one in charge of information. It's probably not standard operating procedure for him to share with me the way he does, but that's his decision. Now the decision has been taken out of his hands."

"You're being awfully mature about this," Thistle said. "If I were in your position, I'd probably be pouting and stomping around until I got my way. Why aren't you?"

I shrugged. "It's not his fault. He has a job to do, rules to follow. I would never forgive myself if he lost his job because of me. He's been in trouble a time or two because I can't stay out of things. He's not in control this go-around, and I think that bothers him on a level he's not willing to admit. If I push him, I'll make things worse."

Thistle's expression was dubious. "Like I said, you're suddenly mature. I'm not a fan of the change."

I laughed as the wind chimes over the door jangled to signify someone's entrance. If it were a customer, I'd gladly volunteer my services to help so Clove and Thistle could finish their lunch. We were between tourist arrivals, though, so if it was a customer it would be a straggler. Instead of a strange face, I found Aunt Tillie staring at us with incredulity.

"What are you three lazybones doing here?" She strode toward the comfortable living room setup at the center of the store. "Why aren't you out gathering information?"

Thistle bit into her sandwich instead of answering. Clove merely pretended she didn't hear the question. That left me to do the heavy lifting.

"What information are we supposed to be gathering?" I asked, legitimately curious. "Has something happened we're not aware of?"

"Um ... yes."

I waited for her to expound. I wasn't disappointed.

"Hemlock Cove is being taken over by alien invaders," she barked. "Don't you understand? We're under attack."

"Oh, well, that's terrible," Thistle drawled. "Are they the warm and fuzzy types from E.T. or the rip-your-face-off types from Alien? We need to know if we need flamethrowers or Reese's Pieces."

"Your wit astounds me," Aunt Tillie deadpanned, her face flushed with color. "Have I ever told you how much I appreciate your mind?"

"As a matter of fact, you haven't."

"There's a reason for that," she barked. "Your mind is often empty ... and always a dangerous place to visit."

"And you are a true joy," Thistle shot back. "How many other people can claim great-aunts who warn about the impending alien invasion? You're a special, special woman." She turned to me, deadpan. "We should call the men with the white coats. She's clearly fried her circuits."

I shot Thistle a quelling look before focusing on Aunt Tillie. "It's not a spaceship."

"It is."

"It's not." I was firm as I shook my head. "It's a drone. I'm convinced of that. I think they were practicing some maneuvers and accidentally crashed. They've got people out in that field searching for stuff. I'm guessing they removed the big wreckage last night when we were sleeping. It was a mistake not to go back then, but it's too late to fix that."

Aunt Tillie was officially intrigued as she shuffled over to sit in the empty chair on the other side of the coffee table. "How do you know they're out there searching?"

"I checked on the site this morning."

"But how did you get out there? I tried to visit, too, but they've got the road cut off with a vehicle. They also have people roaming in the woods. It's not impossible to get past them, but it's not easy. They're all talking on headsets and checking in with one another every few minutes, so you can't take one out without risking the others coming to look for you."

I was flabbergasted. "I see you've given this a lot of thought."

Aunt Tillie simply shrugged. "I wasn't going to kill anybody, so don't worry about that. I was simply going to knock them out. I had potions in my pocket, and I ordered nunchucks from Amazon and was hoping to get a chance to use them."

Thistle choked on her sandwich she laughed so hard. "Nunchucks? You can buy nunchucks on Amazon?"

"You can buy anything on Amazon."

"Good to know." Thistle widened her eyes as she snagged my gaze. "Definitely call the men with the straitjackets. It's time Aunt Tillie went bye-bye."

I ignored her tone and instead focused on eliciting information from Aunt Tillie. "How close did you get?"

"Not close enough to see the field. It sounds like you had better luck. They have a lot of special agent dudes running around the woods. That proves they're looking for aliens."

"How do you figure that?" Clove asked, balling up her sandwich wrapping and placing it on the table. "They could be looking for pieces of a drone like Bay says. I mean, if it's an experimental aircraft, they won't want anyone getting their hands on the technology. That makes more sense than aliens, doesn't it?"

Aunt Tillie never met a rational argument she didn't want to immediately dismiss. "No. You're falling for 'The Man's' line. I always taught you not to fall for that. Have my efforts been in vain?"

"Calm down, Esmerelda," I soothed, shaking my head. "There's no reason to get dramatic."

"I'm not being dramatic. I'm being smart." Aunt Tillie tapped her temple for emphasis. "My brain is the same size as yours, but it's enhanced so I understand things better."

"Did the aliens do that?" Thistle asked dryly. "Did they kidnap you, transfer you to their ship and enhance your brain? That seems like a weird way to prove their superior capabilities."

"Oh, ye of little faith." Aunt Tillie rolled her eyes so hard I was surprised she didn't fall off the chair. "I would be exactly the sort of person to entice aliens to visit."

I couldn't wait to hear this. "Why is that?"

Thistle made an exaggerated face. "Why did you ask her that? We don't need to hear the answer. It's going to be stupid."

Aunt Tillie ignored Thistle's outburst. "The reason aliens would be attracted to me is because I live in the middle of nowhere and I stand out in a crowd of idiots and non-believers. I'm the perfect specimen."

"What does living in the middle of nowhere have to do with anything?" Clove queried. "Wouldn't it be easier to find specimens in urban areas? The population is denser there."

"There might be more people, but there's no place to land a spaceship in a city," Aunt Tillie replied knowingly. "You need a field to land a spaceship."

"Good to know in case we ever need to send you back to your home planet," Thistle drawled.

This time Aunt Tillie couldn't push forward without acknowledging Thistle's attitude. "You're on my list."

Thistle shrugged. "What else is new?"

"If it weren't for the government agents out to cover up what could be the biggest story ever, you would be at the top of my list," Aunt Tillie grumbled. "As it stands, you're relatively safe because there are bigger douches out there to worry about at the present time."

"Well, I'm so glad not to be the head douche." Thistle beamed and puffed out her chest. "I think I might get a T-shirt made up that says 'Middling Douche' and wear it with pride."

I had to bite the inside of my cheek to keep from laughing. "I think you should definitely get the shirt."

"And I think you guys are being purposely obtuse," Aunt Tillie challenged, fire in her eyes. "Think about it. Why would the government be trying to cover up a crash in a field if aliens weren't involved?"

"I already told you that I think it's a drone and they don't want anyone seeing the technology," I answered calmly. "Maybe there was something else on the drone. I mean ... that smell had to come from somewhere. I think it's far more likely they had a biological agent on the drone and they don't want anyone finding out because residents will make a big stink about it."

"What kind of biological agent?" Clove asked, serious. "You said the guy had burns on his hands. What if it's something that could kill us?"

That hadn't occurred to me, but it should have. "I don't know. If it's something dangerous, Landon and Chief Terry wouldn't keep it a secret. Even though they're good at their jobs and don't want to leave them, they wouldn't put the populace at risk. They're good men."

"I agree with Bay there, but what if Landon and Chief Terry don't know the whole truth?" Thistle countered. "Landon is used to being in charge. His nose is out of joint because he has zero control. That Agent Gibson guy was a real turd. What if he wanted us out of there so we didn't get contaminated and he simply didn't tell Landon and Chief Terry his real concern? I can see him doing that."

Sadly, so could I. "So, what do you think they're doing in the field? Do you think they're searching for chemicals?"

"I have no idea. This is out of my area of expertise."

"That's why you have me," Aunt Tillie interjected. "I know exactly what they're looking for."

"If you say aliens, I'm going to tell our mothers and you'll finally be locked up in a home where you belong," Thistle warned.

"Hey, you don't know it's not aliens." Aunt Tillie refused to back down. It was hardly a new occurrence. That's how she rolled. "It's just as likely to be aliens as it is to be a drone."

"I think I'm going to have to side with Bay on this one," Clove hedged. "I don't think it's aliens."

"You just don't want it to be aliens," Aunt Tillie grumbled. "You're still traumatized from the time I showed you *Predator*. You were supposed to learn survival skills from that movie. Instead, you cried for three days straight."

Clove's eyebrows flew up her forehead. "There were skinned bodies in that movie! Oh, and exploded heads ... and hearts being ripped out ... and skulls being ripped out ... and arms being cut off ... and a bunch of other gross stuff."

"Pfft." Aunt Tillie was hearing none of it. "That movie is a classic.

It's also based on a real-life event that the government doesn't want us to know about. There are files and everything, but the government hides them."

"This is really going too far," Thistle mumbled. "I mean ... come on."

As if on cue — perhaps the universe understood Thistle needed a break from Aunt Tillie's theories — the store door opened again. This time the person who entered gave me a hard jolt. I couldn't remember the last time I'd seen this face in Hypnotic.

"Mrs. Little?" Clove's forehead puckered as she slowly stood. "I ... do you need something?"

Thistle was less excited about the visit. "If you're here to complain because we didn't scrub the sides of the dumpster in the alley with Clorox again, then you can turn right around and walk out. We're not doing that. It smells like that because that's where the trash lives until the trucks show up to cart it away. The tourists don't go into the alley anyway."

Mrs. Little either didn't understand or didn't hear. Instead of reacting as she normally would — with a scowl and glare — she smiled as her gaze bounced between faces. "It's a lovely day, isn't it?"

"What's going on?" Thistle was instantly on guard as she straightened and glanced around the store. "Are we on a hidden camera show? If so, I'm going to start throwing punches. You know how I feel about reality television."

Mrs. Little let loose a low chuckle. "Oh, Thistle. You're always so funny. You have a delightful sense of humor. Has anyone ever told you that?"

"Not you."

"Well, I've always thought it." Mrs. Little smoothed her hands over her skirt as she focused on Aunt Tillie. "It's so good to see you in town. You don't stop by nearly enough. I miss seeing you. We should have tea in the bakery while you're here. You know, catch up."

Aunt Tillie's mouth dropped open. "Did someone lace my doughnuts with acid this morning?"

"As much as I would like to call the men in white coats to collect you, I can't on this one," Thistle responded. "The old lady has gone batshit crazy. Er, even crazier than before. It was bound to happen but ... wow! It really came out of nowhere."

"See?" Mrs. Little's smile was so wide it threatened to swallow her entire face. She pointed at Thistle and giggled. "So funny. She could do a standup routine and pull in millions of dollars if she wanted."

I was beyond baffled at the turn of the events. "Mrs. Little, are you feeling okay?"

"I've never felt better, dear. I feel like a woman of forty again. Of course, that's only a few years younger than my actual age."

Mrs. Little was in her eighties, like Aunt Tillie — they went to high school together. "Well ... ."

"I told you." Aunt Tillie folded her arms across her chest and made a tsking sound with her tongue. "It's aliens. It's not the fun type either. This is exactly what I was afraid of."

"You've lost me," Thistle said. "What's the fun type?"

"The ones who would've skinned her alive."

"Fair enough." Thistle nodded encouragingly. "Continue."

"It's as I feared," Aunt Tillie's tone turned grave, "it's the sort of aliens who crawl into your ears and take over your personality."

"So ... *Invasion of the Body Snatchers*?" I asked.

Aunt Tillie shook her head. "No. Worse. *Star Trek II*."

"Oh, *The Wrath of Khan*."

"Yes." Aunt Tillie was deathly serious. "Batten down the hatches. Spock is about to die."

"Spock isn't real," Thistle pointed out.

Aunt Tillie's scowl was back. "It was a metaphor. Can't you ever just let me say what I want to say without being a pain in the butt?"

"It's a stupid metaphor," Thistle complained.

I barely kept one ear on their argument as I focused on Mrs. Little. Her smile never wavered. She seemed to be enjoying the show, if she even understood it.

"So, where did we land on that tea?" Mrs. Little asked finally. "I would love to spend some quality time with you, Tillie."

"Set phasers on stun," Clove intoned, leaning forward. "I'm starting to think Aunt Tillie's alien theory makes sense."

Sadly, I couldn't entirely push it out of my mind either. What a freaking day.

ALIEN INSPIRATION

> Does anyone ever worry that Aunt Tillie will somehow make the movie *Cocoon* a reality? Imagine if she actually managed to reverse the signs of aging. She could legitimately outlive us. That is a terrifying thought. Yeah … we definitely need to keep Aunt Tillie from meeting aliens. It will mean the end for us.
> **Thistle vents her frustration with Aunt Tillie**

SEVEN

FROM HEMLOCK COVE ... A WARNING AND AN ULTIMATUM.

I spent the next hour pretending I couldn't hear what Aunt Tillie said while keeping watch on the police station. A constant stream of words escaped my great-aunt's mouth — each one more ridiculous than the previous statement — and a constant stream of people parked at the station, went inside and then left.

It seemed suspicious and I was bothered because I had absolutely no idea what was going on.

"If we're going to fight aliens, I think we should all take on personas," Aunt Tillie noted as she munched on a bag of potato chips supplied by Clove. "I want to be Ripley. She's the biggest badass of the group."

Clove, who was much more interested in chick flicks than science fiction, wrinkled her nose. "Who is Ripley?"

Aunt Tillie made an exaggerated face. "Are you serious?"

Clove merely blinked.

"You're out of the family," Aunt Tillie hissed. "You've finally done it. You've embarrassed me to the point of no return. I can't even look at you." As if to prove it, she pressed her hand over her eyes and made a series of distressed sounds as she swung her legs back and forth on the chair. "Who is Ripley? I mean ... are you trying to kill me?"

Instead of responding to Aunt Tillie, Clove shifted her gaze to me. "Who is Ripley?"

"Sigourney Weaver in the *Alien* movies," I answered, my eyes still on the police station. "Five different vehicles have parked across the way in the past hour. Five different men entered the building and then left again. None of the vehicles are marked. Don't you find that weird?"

Aunt Tillie nodded without hesitation. "That's how 'The Man' operates. They're over there plotting how they're going to keep the aliens secret. They don't care that the aliens want to kill us. They only care that we don't find out the aliens want to kill us."

Thistle, who had moved to the floor so she could continue sorting herbs, was blasé. "See, I don't get the aliens wanting to kill us thing. Why travel millions of light years to visit Earth and immediately decide to attack?"

"You don't know it's immediate," Aunt Tillie countered. "It could be like *War of the Worlds*. They could've planted big ships — or crawlers, whatever those things were — in the ground and decided to awaken them because they watched long enough to realize we deserve to die.

"I mean, think about it," she continued. "What if you were an alien, a superior being from another planet, and you came to Earth and the first thing you saw was a Kardashian? Or Margaret Little, for that matter?"

I finally dragged my eyes from the police station and focused on Aunt Tillie. "Where is your new buddy? I thought you were going to meet her for tea."

"No, I told her I'd call her and we'd set up a date for tea," Aunt Tillie clarified. "Then I sent her back to play with her unicorns while I figure out exactly what she's up to. It's not good, by the way. I've narrowed it down to three things."

"Do we want to know those three things?" I asked dryly.

"I don't." Clove vehemently shook her head. "Whenever we know the things, we end up in trouble. I don't want to be in trouble. Sam and I are grilling tonight for the first time this season, and if there's trouble I won't get my steak."

Clove's live-in boyfriend Sam had been good for her in many ways. He listened to her, encouraged her and even stood up for her during family battles. He also coddled her, which made Clove even more of a whiner than she had been while growing up. It was annoying.

"I'm going to tell you anyway." Aunt Tillie barreled forward as if Clove hadn't said a word. "Margaret is a master at manipulation. She always has been. My first hunch is that she's working with the rest of the women in town to drive me crazy. They're all jealous because — well, I'm me — and none of them can be me. This is her attempt to lull me into a false sense of security so she can lure me away from town and kill me in the woods."

Thistle tilted her head to the side, considering. "How is she going to kill you?"

"Probably a wood chipper."

"*Fargo?*"

"*Universal Soldier.*"

"Of course." Thistle bobbed her head. "Continue."

"I think this is the most likely scenario, but given what's going on, something else could be afoot," Aunt Tillie enthused. "It's possible that she was taken over by an alien from the crashed ship."

"Except it was a drone," I pointed out.

"Puh-leez." Aunt Tillie rolled her eyes to the sky, as if pleading for the Goddess to make her idiotic great-nieces see the error of their ways. "It was a spaceship. You don't want to admit that — and I get it because you lack imagination and need to believe 'The Man' would never hide something this big from you — but it was definitely a spaceship. The invasion has already begun. It's too late to stop it from happening, but it's not too late to bring it to an end."

"Yeah, yeah." I made a dismissive wave. "We've heard about the invasion. Let it go."

Aunt Tillie had no intention of doing that. "You know darned well the alien invasion is happening. You saw Margaret with your own eyes. She was even loopier than normal, and none of us thought that was possible."

"She was a little nutty," Clove confirmed. "Maybe she has been invaded by aliens."

Oh, geez. This was the last thing I needed. Clove was always the first person in the family to fall for Aunt Tillie's wild theories. Twila would be next. Then Thistle would start with the "maybe she's right" crap. Ultimately, I'd be the only one standing firm. Okay, I wouldn't stand firm. I'd fall victim to the hysteria and we'd all do something stupid together. That's the Winchester way, and things weren't suddenly going to cease following normal patterns now.

"She hasn't been invaded by aliens," Thistle snapped.

"How would you explain it?" Aunt Tillie challenged. "Bay said she was out at the field yesterday. Something weird is happening at that crash site. Now Margaret is acting friendly, when we all know that she wouldn't be nice to us if someone had a gun to her head. There's only one explanation."

"Aliens, right?" My temper was threatening to fray. "Last time I checked it was the sort of aliens from *Invasion of the Body Snatchers*, right?"

"Mock all you want," Aunt Tillie shot back. "I'm right about this. All my preparations are finally going to come to fruition."

I had no idea what that meant. "What preparations?"

"You know. My preparations for the end times."

"I thought you prepared for the zombie apocalypse," I challenged. "I don't remember you preparing for an alien invasion."

"I thought she prepared for when the electrical grid failed," Thistle countered. "That's when the Russians nuke us, right?"

"Not just the Russians." Aunt Tillie pinned Thistle with a dark look. "Don't be absurd. The Russians don't have the power to do it themselves. North Korea helps."

"Of course."

"And Canada."

I stilled. "Wait ... Canada is attacking our power grid? Why? They're nice – and they like us."

Aunt Tillie waved me off with a dismissive gesture. "Don't you know an act when you see one? They're setting us up. They're playing the long game. They're putting drugs in our maple syrup to control our minds."

"Uh-huh." This conversation was getting old. "Let's go back to talking about the people going in and out of the police station. What government agency do you think they're from?"

Aunt Tillie had no intention of ceding her current spot as center of the universe. "I'm telling you that Margaret Little has been invaded by aliens, and I'm prepared to take them down."

"I think you'll do a masterful job of it," Clove said enthusiastically. "I'm glad that you've prepared."

"Yes, I'm glad you've prepared," Thistle drawled. "Is that why you've been hanging around Hank in the woods?"

Aunt Tillie adopted an innocent expression. "I have no idea what you're talking about."

"The weird prepper who lives in the woods," Thistle pressed. "We all know you've seen him a time or two at the very least. Do you want to know how we know? He told us. Yup. He told us you visit him all the time."

"I don't know if he said 'all the time,'" Clove hedged. "He did say he sees you occasionally."

"Well, Hank William Jenkins has a big mouth," Aunt Tillie challenged. "He's also not very bright. I mean ... his mother named him Hank William Jenkins. How weird is that?"

"We're named after herbs," I pointed out.

"Be glad no one named you garlic and shut up about that," Aunt Tillie warned. "Do you have any idea how sick I am of hearing about that?"

"Not as sick as we are of being named after herbs," Thistle shot back.

"Ugh. I'm done." Aunt Tillie held up her hands. "I can't believe you idiots are on my alien invasion team. I should've picked better."

"Yes, well, you'll know better for next time." I slowly got to my feet and walked to the door. "I'm heading over to the police station before going home. I want to see what they're up to over there."

"I thought Landon warned you not to get involved in the police side of things this time," Clove argued. "Won't he be angry if he sees you?"

I shrugged. "He'll get over it. It's not as if we're going to break up because I poked my nose into an investigation. If that was the rule, we wouldn't have made it to our third date."

"She has a point." Aunt Tillie said sagely.

I paused with my hand on the door knob and turned back to face her. "You said there were three possibilities for why Mrs. Little was acting weird. What's the third?"

"That she's trying to irritate me just to irritate me," Aunt Tillie replied.

"Oh, well, that's it," Thistle said.

"That's definitely it," Clove agreed.

"I'm going with the third option," I offered.

Aunt Tillie's expression was withering. "Seriously, how did you guys end up on my alien invasion team? This is just the worst."

I LEFT THISTLE AND CLOVE to deal with Aunt Tillie's alien invasion delusions and headed for the police station. It was a small building — only two entrances — and I figured walking through the front door was a mistake. Chief Terry's secretary was often bothered by my presence, and if Agent Gibson was inside he was most likely working in the small conference room at the front of the building. The people I was interested in talking to were at the back of the building.

I lucked out upon entering. The building was mostly quiet, no one loitering in the hallway. I heard people talking at the other end of the corridor, but I didn't recognize the voices. That meant it was probably Agent Gibson's team. I wasn't interested in hearing what they had to say ... at least for now.

The low voices I heard in Chief Terry's office were of more interest to me. I recognized both right away, and they didn't sound happy.

"He won't let me see the report from the hospital," Landon said. The door to Chief Terry's office was cracked, but I still had to strain to hear. If someone walked into the hallway and saw me, I'd be in a lot of trouble. That didn't dissuade me from listening. I was so curious there was almost nothing that could yank me from my current plan of attack.

"What do you think he's hiding in that report?" Chief Terry asked.

"You know what I think he's hiding." Landon sounded weary. I couldn't see his face, but I recognized the tone. He was tired and crabby, never a good combination. "He's in charge, yet he's keeping us almost completely in the dark. I don't like it."

"What other options do we have?" Always a pragmatic soul, Chief Terry was calm as he asked the question. "You're not in charge of this one. Oh, don't make that face. I didn't say it to irritate you. No, really. I would much rather have you in charge than that ... asshat."

Landon snorted. "You picked up that word from Bay."

"Actually, Bay picked up that word from Marnie back in the day," Chief Terry corrected. "The girls used it for a long time, although I think Bay is the only one who still uses it."

"You know, sometimes it annoys me that you know more about my girlfriend than I do," Landon groused.

"I don't know more about her. I've simply known her longer. I can guarantee that you know more about her than I do. And, no, I don't want to know what those things are. You're perverted enough in my head that I can barely tolerate things as it is."

Now it was Landon's turn to be amused. "Oh, now, don't be like that. You love me, and you know it."

"Very rarely do I love you."

"You love Bay."

"I do love Bay."

"She loves me."

"Which is the only reason you're not dead," Chief Terry fired back, causing me to smile at his gruff tone. His bark may be worse than his bite, but in fact, he has no bite. He's a big marshmallow, especially where Winchester witches are concerned. He doted on us, spoiled us. He also disciplined us when things fell apart on the home front. He always did his best for us, something I'll never forget.

"I think you talk big, but you really like me." Landon heaved out a sigh. I could practically see him in my head. I knew how he looked when he was tired. He would be rubbing his forehead ... and maybe the back of his neck. He would be shifting in his chair. "I don't know what to do about this situation. I don't like it."

"I don't like it either," Chief Terry admitted. "It's not just the fact that they're keeping something from us — and I'm against that on general principle because we're supposed to be working together — but it's also the fact that weird things are going on."

"A lot of weird things," Landon agreed. "There are so many weird things going on I'm afraid that Bay will stumble over something and turn it into a huge ordeal."

"She's definitely digging," Chief Terry said. "She won't let up. You know that, don't you? She'll go deep until she finds what she's looking for."

"I know." Landon almost sounded petulant. "It's pure torture knowing she's running around out there. How close do you think she got to that field?"

"I don't know. She's familiar with the area. It's possible she got a lot closer than Gibson's men believe."

"Gibson's men didn't see her today," Landon said. "I know she was out there, though. Her shoes were filthy."

"Tillie was out there. She was sighted twice. The men were laughing about her antics. They said she was a harmless little old lady wandering in the woods."

Landon snorted. "They have a surprise coming."

"I'm almost looking forward to Tillie taking them on," Chief Terry admitted. "That doesn't mean I like cutting Bay out of this. I'm not used to it, and the more it happens, the more determined she'll be to get a story."

"I told Gibson that," Landon argued. "I told him he needs to share something with her if he wants her to go away. He won't listen. He thinks Bay is some cute little weekly reporter who will simply obey orders."

"We know better."

"I don't like being separated from her on stuff like this," Landon said. "She tends to dive in headfirst on these things. I hate that I can't be there if she needs me. I mean ... I really hate it."

"Bay took care of herself long before you showed up," Chief Terry supplied. "She'll be okay."

"I know that, but it's different now. She can ... well, she can do more than she could do even a few weeks ago."

Chief Terry made an odd throat-clearing sound. "You know, I don't like to talk about stuff like that. The ... weird stuff. We should let that go for the time being."

"Fine. I don't know what to say about it anyway."

"Great. Um ... back to work. I don't see how we can move forward if Gibson won't tell us exactly what we're dealing with."

"Maybe we should press him again," Landon suggested. "He'll probably say no, but there's no harm in asking."

"Fair enough."

I heard feet shuffling on the floor and scurried away from the door, ducking around the corner to hide before Landon and Chief Terry hit the hallway.

"I want to tell Bay the truth," Landon admitted as they exited Chief Terry's office. "I don't have a problem telling her because I know she won't print it in the newspaper. Gibson has other ideas."

"If I had my druthers, I'd tell her, too. But we're not in charge."

"That doesn't mean I have to like it."

"Join the club. We have no choice. For this one, at least, Bay is on her own."

"That's exactly what I'm afraid of."

ALIEN INSPIRATION

> If these guys can kill each other with glowing sticks why would they ever do anything but hack off heads and call it a day? Although, to be fair, that mind-choking thing they can do is cool, too. I would love that power. Maybe I should become a Jedi.

Thistle makes the mistake of watching *Star Wars* while suffering from PMS

EIGHT

OCEANS RISE. CITIES FALL. MAGIC SURVIVES.

Landon met me at the guesthouse before dinner. He looked beaten down when he entered, but he mustered a smile when he saw I hadn't yet left for the inn.

"Hey."

"Hi." I felt uncomfortable. Generally, eavesdropping didn't fill me with such guilt. This time was different. We were at odds, and it was nothing we'd created. Outside forces were at play, which meant we weren't sabotaging ourselves. I should have been comforted by that. It didn't quite work out that way, though. "How was your day?"

"Long." Landon tossed his keys on the console table by the door. "Yours?"

"Long."

He grinned. "I'm a little sad that's all we can share."

"Me, too. We'll get through it." I had faith in that. We'd been through much worse. "They put together a taco bar at the inn tonight. That should perk us up."

"There's nothing tacos can't fix." Landon cupped the back of my head and gave me a soft, lingering kiss. "How about we eat fast and then come back here? I could use some quiet time tonight, just you and me."

He wasn't the only one. "Sounds like a plan."

"Good. Don't put any onions on your tacos. It might ruin the plan."

"I'll consider it."

THE INN WAS DEVOID of guests until the following day, so the parking lot was empty. I was glad for it. We let ourselves in through the back door, the one that led to the family living quarters. I wasn't surprised to find it quiet. Other than Aunt Tillie, everyone was in the kitchen preparing dinner.

"What are you doing?" Landon asked when he realized Aunt Tillie was at the small table in the corner of the room rather than her usual perch in front of the television.

"Making plans," Aunt Tillie replied, refusing to look up from her task. "Someone has to be in charge of this thing. I'm best suited, so the responsibility falls to me."

Landon flicked his eyes to me. "Do I even want to know what she's talking about?"

"Alien invasion," I answered automatically.

"Ah." Landon merely shook his head. "What aliens are we fighting?"

Aunt Tillie didn't answer. Apparently she couldn't concentrate and ramp up the snark at the same time. That meant she really was interested in whatever she toiled over.

"*Invasion of the Body Snatchers*," I answered for her. "That's the only thing that explains why Mrs. Little is acting out of sorts."

"Chief Terry visited her," Landon offered. "He said she seemed fine, didn't have trouble making eye contact and knew when and where she was. He didn't think there was anything to worry about."

Hmm. That was interesting. "When did he see her?"

Landon shrugged. "After you told us she was acting weird. That was at lunch, so not long after."

"Well, she stopped in at Hypnotic after that," I said. "She was definitely acting weird. She invited Aunt Tillie for tea and doughnuts at the bakery."

Landon's mouth dropped open. "Was she serious?"

"She seemed to be."

"Is there a chance she could've poisoned the tea and doughnuts?"

"I hadn't even considered it. That's plausible. You should add that to your list, Aunt Tillie."

Instead of firing off a snappy comeback, Aunt Tillie simply nodded. "Okay. That sounds fine. I'll do that."

Landon and I exchanged weighted — and amused — looks.

"Well, we'll let you get back to your plotting," Landon said finally. "If you need help finding a scientist to create a cure for the virus, let me know. I'll point you in the right direction."

I lifted an eyebrow as Landon pointed me toward the kitchen. "Virus?"

"I saw that movie," Landon explained. "Nicole Kidman, right?"

"That was like the fourth movie," I corrected. "There were three others before it."

"So? They all end the same way, right?"

I shook my head. "The first three movies have downer endings. There is no stopping the alien invasion in them. It's impossible. The world gets taken over by the pods."

Landon furrowed his brow. "That doesn't sound very upbeat."

"I don't believe it's meant to be upbeat."

"Well, thankfully the pod people are only in Aunt Tillie's mind. You don't have to worry about that."

"Good point."

We left Aunt Tillie to her alien invasion battle plan, stopped in the kitchen long enough to talk to my mother and aunts, and then hit the dining room. Sam, Clove, Marcus and Thistle were already seated when we entered.

"I didn't know you guys were coming for dinner tonight," I noted as Landon poured two glasses of wine. "Did they suck you in with the taco bar, too?"

"That and Clove wants to make sure none of the aliens have taken over family members," Sam said dryly. "She won't let it go ... even though I told her it was ludicrous."

Ah, we were right on schedule. Aunt Tillie had managed to work her magic on Clove. That meant Twila was next. "Well, it's not really her fault," I offered. "We spent the better part of the afternoon with Aunt Tillie. She's very convincing when she wants to be."

"She's a menace," Sam argued. "Clove spent an entire hour checking all the door and window locks. Do you have any idea how long she's going to keep me up tonight?"

"Sounds promising," Landon offered.

"Then I'm telling the story wrong." Sam scowled. "You don't understand. Clove gets ... worked up ... about stuff like this. I've had to talk her down from her Bigfoot fear at least five times since she moved in. Bay doesn't get like this, so you have no idea what it's like."

"Bay has her own brand of lunacy," Landon countered. "You'll learn to deal with it. I mean ... if she's up and has a lot of energy the answer is to turn that energy into another activity."

I slid him a sidelong look. "You're probably not going to want to mention anything like that in front of our mothers."

"Duly noted."

"Besides, I can't be distracted," Clove said, her eyes fierce. "I've been giving it a lot of thought. I think Aunt Tillie is right. It's aliens. That explains the guy with the burned hands Bay saw. It explains all the secrets. What else could it be?"

I cringed when Landon's hand landed on my back. It was large and warm, and usually I found comfort in a simple tactile exchange such as this. I knew that wouldn't be the case tonight. "What guy with burned hands?"

Uh-oh. I scorched Clove with a dark look. "You have such a big mouth."

Clove wasn't apologetic in the least. "Hey, we're being invaded by aliens. The size of my mouth has nothing to do with that."

"It will if we shove something in your mouth to shut you up," Thistle countered.

"Don't you care that aliens are probably taking over people we know all over town?" Clove challenged, her voice going shrill. "How can you not care about that?"

"Oh, man." Sam slapped his hand to his forehead. "I think I need to get drunk."

"If you do, you're stuck here for the night," Thistle said. "Are you sure that's what you want?"

"It might be easier to foist her off on everyone else so I can get some sleep." Sam looked resigned. "Seriously, where's the whiskey?"

"It looks like Sam is going to get drunk," I said to Landon. "That might be fun. Do you want to join in?"

"No." Landon's eyes flashed with warning when they locked with mine. "What guy with burns did you tell your cousins about?"

Crap. I was going to kill Clove. Aliens were the least of her worries. "You know how she is. She makes things up. She freaks out over nothing. She doesn't know what she's talking about."

"Except she was very specific this time," Landon pressed. "Were you out at the scene today?"

He already knew the answer to that. "I have no idea what you're talking about."

Landon's lips curved down. "Bay ... ."

"Hey, you can't push her to answer your questions when you won't answer hers," Thistle interjected, her temper on full display. "Relationships are give and take. You're not giving anything, so you can't take anything."

"That was almost profound, Thistle," Landon drawled. "But you're not part of this conversation. I was talking to Bay."

"She's right," I argued. "I can't tell you what I was doing this afternoon."

"Who said that? When did that become the rule? You most certainly can tell me what you were doing this afternoon."

I sucked in a calming breath. A riotous fight between the entire family would not help matters. "You can't share information with me."

"I'm under orders not to."

"That means I can't share information with you. We've already discussed this."

"We've discussed that you won't – not can't, but won't – share information with me as payback," Landon clarified. "There's a big difference."

"That doesn't change the fact that we're in something of a quandary." I refused to back down. "You're the one who said we both have jobs to do."

"And now I'm totally regretting it," Landon complained. "Can't you just let it go?"

"Can you?"

"I ... ." He worked his jaw, his expression unreadable. Finally, he threw up his hands and shook his head. "I refuse to let this derail us. I get that you're upset because I can't share information with you. I don't blame you. I can't help the way you want me to help."

"I'm not pressing you for information. I've been good."

"You have been ... for the most part. You've gotten a few passive-aggressive digs in, but that's to be expected."

"So ... what's the problem?"

"The problem is that I don't like not being able to share every aspect of my life with you," Landon answered. "I mean, I never talked with you about cases you weren't involved in — and you never asked, which I'm grateful for — but I miss working with you."

I wanted to be angry, but it wasn't easy when he opened himself and invited potential ridicule. "I hate this." I rubbed my forehead. "I can't wait until this over."

"Oh, the aliens are never going to leave," Clove said. "It can't end unless we end it."

Landon spared her a glance. "Maybe someone should cut her off."

"Nope." Sam shook his head. "We're staying here and getting drunk. That's the only way I can get through this."

Landon snorted. "Good luck with that." He slowly tracked his gaze back to me. "I don't know how you got out there today — and don't bother denying you did because it's not worth the aggravation — but you need to be careful."

"Because you're worried I'll get burned?"

"Because I'm worried about all of it," Landon admitted. "You think

I'm keeping stuff from you, but in truth, I know very little. You'd be surprised how little I really know."

I remembered his conversation with Chief Terry, and my heart gave a sigh. "It'll be okay. I promise. Don't worry about me."

"Worry goes with the job description." He poured himself more wine. "I'm starting to think Sam's plan to get hammered might be a good one."

"You won't feel that way tomorrow when you have to go to work."

"Good point." He drank half his glass. "You don't think it's aliens, do you?"

"Of course not. It's a government drone. Perhaps there was a chemical onboard that no one is supposed to know about because it could cause sickness … and death … and possibly mutations."

Landon's eyebrows shifted. "I don't think that's much better, Bay."

"I guess it depends on how you look at it."

"And how are you looking at it?"

"With the most analytical eye I can."

"I guess I can't ask for more than that." Landon briefly pressed his forehead to mine. "Don't get in trouble, Bay. I'm terrified I won't be able to get you out of whatever you stumble over. Be careful."

"I'm always careful."

"Be way more careful than that."

IT WAS ALMOST MIDNIGHT when I slipped out of bed. Landon snored lightly, the covers drawn around him as he slept on his side. He was dead to the world … and would stay that way if I had anything to say about it.

I lightly rested my fingers on his forehead, murmuring as I planted a lullaby in his mind. It was a spell Aunt Tillie had taught me. I'd been caught casting it once before — and Landon hadn't been happy — but I was more adept at it now. I was certain it would work this time.

We had a problem we couldn't escape. He loved his job and believed he was doing good work. I believed that, too. Mostly he worked crime scenes and took down murderers. This time he was doing someone else's bidding ... and he hated it. That didn't mean he wouldn't follow orders. He would, even if it took a toll on him. Because I loved him, I didn't want him to put his job at risk. It would break his heart to lose his position, and that was the last thing I wanted.

On the flip side, I couldn't stop myself from being curious. I didn't consider myself a conspiracy theorist — I left that to Aunt Tillie — or an alarmist. Clove had us covered on that front, after all. I couldn't simply walk away from what I knew, though. Something — whether an airplane or drone — went down in that field. Now the federal government was trying to cover it up. That didn't sit right with me.

Landon knew me well enough to understand I couldn't let it go. He wasn't the type to ask me to curb my instincts to make him more comfortable. Sure, he worried about me. Sometimes I thought he worried too much. Then I realized the real reason he worried, and it dulled the leading edge of my agitation. He worried because he loved me, which sometimes felt miraculous. He also worried because he'd seen some of the worst things this world had to offer through his job, and he wanted to protect me from that. It wasn't a terrible inclination.

Part of me wanted to walk away from the story because it would've been easier on both of us, but that wasn't in my nature. I had to see.

So, I planted a lullaby in Landon's head to make sure he wouldn't wake up. He needed a good night's sleep. Then I slipped out of the guesthouse and headed toward the access road that led to the field on foot. It was only a mile and a half away if I cut through the trees. If Clove was with me, that wouldn't have been an option because of her Bigfoot fear. I was alone, though, and I wasn't afraid.

Okay, I was mildly afraid. It wasn't the woods that frightened me; it was the possibility of running into federal agents. I had to be really careful ... and quiet. I wasn't sure if I would be able to see anything. But I had to look, and it was safer to look at night.

I followed a path I knew. For years, Clove, Thistle and I had played in these woods. We were knights storming a castle, and *G.I. Joe* agents saving the day, and occasionally the Crocodile Hunter because ... well, he was just awesome. There were no crocodiles to hunt, but we enjoyed pretending.

Tonight, I was simply Bay Winchester and I was on a mission.

I made most of the trip in relative silence. The normal sounds of the forest didn't frighten me. I knew the animals that lived there, mostly opossums, raccoons and the occasional coyote. A few people swore up and down that a mountain lion had been seen in the area, but I didn't believe that. The bear sightings were more troublesome, but I learned at a young age that as long as you stayed away from a bear's cubs you were fine.

It wasn't until I was almost to Potter's Field that the normal woodsy concert given by owls and bugs gave way to different noises. Instinctively, I ducked behind a tree and focused on the field. Lighting was an issue for obvious reasons, but some sort of flood lamps had been moved into the field. They were pointed directly at the charred earth, and at least ten people appeared to be walking a search grid — exactly like the one I saw a few hours before — across the property.

I inched closer, resting a hand on a tree trunk as I tried to get a better look. I was lost in the scene in front of me, but that didn't mean I forgot the area behind. When a twig snapped, my body stiffened. I knew I wasn't alone, but it was already too late when a hand covered my mouth and snapped my body back.

"You're in so much trouble."

ALIEN INSPIRATION

> Landon fancies himself Han Solo, but there's no way that's how it would shake out if this were a *Star Wars* movie. I've got it all figured out. I would be Han Solo. Thistle would be Chewbacca. Winnie would be Princess Leia because she's good at being bossy. Marcus would be Lando because he's chill … and then some. Clove would be R2D2 because she's small and I don't understand half of what comes out of her mouth. Twila would be an Ewok because there are times I think she would take a rock to a laser gun fight. Bay would be Luke Skywalker because she's a whiner. Marnie would be Boba Fett because she's willing to sell people out when she's in a bad mood. That leaves Landon to be C3P0. He likes to be everyone's moral compass, so it fits. He also walks like he's got a certain something-something gumming up the works. Now, if we could only find his "off" switch.
> **Aunt Tillie breaking down *Star Wars***

NINE

SHE IS NOT AFRAID. SHE IS NOT ALONE. SHE IS TWO BLOCKS FROM THE INN.

My heart thudded as I slapped at the hand. Then the words, the tone and the voice infiltrated my head and I widened my eyes.

"I mean ... a lot of trouble, Bay," Landon growled, keeping his hand in place over my mouth so I couldn't respond as he dragged me lower into the foliage. "I can't believe you thought that lullaby thing was going to work a second time. And REO Speedwagon? Really? You thought I would dream about that dreck?"

I managed to wrench his hand from my mouth and shifted so I could see his face. He was dressed in black jogging pants and hoodie, his hair swept back from his face. He looked furious.

Despite that, I was glad to see him. "I planted that song because it's romantic. You know, that part about loving you forever and stuff. I wanted you to sleep well."

Landon shook his head. "That won't work."

"I do love you."

"Oh, geez." Landon rolled his eyes. "You are ... un-freaking-believable."

I shrugged. "I had to see."

"I know you did. I was expecting this move, if you want to know the truth. I knew you wouldn't be able to let it go. Coming out here at night made the most sense."

"So ... why didn't you try to stop me?"

"Because I'm not your keeper."

"You stalked me in the woods," I pointed out. "That's something a keeper might do."

Landon scowled. "Are you trying to give me an aneurysm?"

"No. I'm trying to see what they're doing. Why are they out here searching in the dark?"

"I don't know." Landon relaxed his grip, though only marginally. I could've attempted to flee but I had nowhere to go. He was behind me, and if I ran forward I'd end up in enemy hands. I was better in his hands. Er, wait, that sounded kind of dirty, didn't it? "I don't understand why they're out here."

Landon was more focused on the search than me now, and something occurred to me. "You let me go without confronting me because you wanted to follow me."

"You're full of it."

"No, it's true." I vehemently shook my head.

"Stop that." Landon forced me lower so he could jerk the hood on my coat over my head. "You should've worn a dark hat, Bay. Your hair stands out. That's how I so easily followed you in the woods."

"You could've made a noise," I complained. "I kept thinking about Bigfoot ... and bears ... and that video of the cougar people say is real. I wouldn't have thought about those things if you'd been with me."

"You deserve to think about those things," Landon fired back. "You cast a spell on me, planted a lullaby in my head so you could more easily lie. And it was a terrible eighties ballad."

"I love that song." I folded my arms over my chest as he tied the hoodie tight so my hair wouldn't spill out. "I always think of you when I hear it on the radio."

"That won't work on me. I'm angry. We're going to talk about this later."

"What are we going to do now?"

"Watch what they're doing, of course." Landon sat on the chilly ground and pulled me into his lap. "Now ... shh."

I studied his profile for a long moment. "This makes it easier for you, doesn't it? I went into the woods and you had to follow because you always feel you need to protect me. If someone catches us, you can always say you were trying to stop me from making it to the scene."

"I wouldn't use that exact excuse. I'd say I woke up, you were gone, and I was worried so I went looking."

"It's the same thing."

"I guess, depending on how you look at it." Landon kept his eyes averted. "You're right that I wanted to see if they were doing something out here. I don't like admitting it because I'm afraid you'll take it as some tacit approval and keep doing things like sneaking through the woods in the middle of the night. That's never a good idea."

"But?" I prodded.

"But I want to see what they're doing, too," Landon admitted. "We didn't know about this. They didn't tell us. There has to be a reason for that."

"You think they're hiding something, don't you?"

"Not aliens."

"I didn't say aliens. I told you my hunch."

"I don't know that I believe your guess either," Landon countered. "I just want to see. I can't hear what they're saying if you keep talking. Besides that, you'll draw attention to us if you don't stop."

"Fine." I snuggled against him, enjoying the way his arms automatically came around me. "Just for the record, I don't think we should fight about this. We were both at fault."

Landon snorted lightly. "Bay, we're going to fight about this."

"Why?"

"I hate REO Speedwagon."

"That's a good band."

"Shh." Landon brushed his lips against my cheek. "I need to see, Bay. Just ... be quiet. That can be your punishment."

"Fine, but I'm going to make you listen to REO Speedwagon later. That'll be your punishment."

"I can't wait."

I FELL ASLEEP.

I wasn't sure when it happened. We watched the workers in the field for a long time. I grew bored after a bit and Landon refused to engage in conversation, so I drifted off. He eventually woke me, placing a hand over my mouth to make sure I didn't speak too loudly.

"We need to go, Bay," he whispered. "They're getting closer to the trees."

"What?" I was confused. "We're still out here?"

He cocked a dark eyebrow. "Did you think I would carry you back? It's more than a mile."

I shrugged. "That would be the gentlemanly thing to do." I made a big show of stretching. "What time is it?"

"After two. We need to go now. I don't want to risk them seeing us."

"Okay." My legs were cramped as I stood, and I had to hold onto his arm to collect my strength. "Did you see anything good?"

"I don't know. They're looking for something."

I'd figured that out myself. "What?"

"I don't know. Come on." He grabbed my hand and pulled me away from the light. "We need to go. Now."

I didn't argue. His tone told me he meant business. I linked my fingers with his and picked up the pace. "I guess we can talk about REO Speedwagon on the way back. They really are underappreciated."

"Yup. You're definitely trying to kill me."

I WOKE BEFORE LANDON, which wasn't surprising. He was hyper-vigilant during the walk home, keeping me pinned to his side as he constantly looked over his shoulder. Even though I wanted to torture him with REO Speedwagon lyrics, his agitation forced me to keep my mouth shut. By the time we returned home we were both exhausted, so we tumbled into bed.

My nap at the crash site gave me an edge, so I got up and showered before him. With nothing better to do, I decided to make breakfast. I wasn't much of a cook — the kitchen witch genes that fueled my mom and aunts skipped my generation — but we had bacon. We always had bacon because it was Landon's version of chocolate. It was the one thing that always put him in a better mood.

I didn't have eggs, hash browns or toast to go with it, but I figured the bacon was a nice side dish for the instant oatmeal I planned to prepare. Anything was better than heading up to the inn and watching Clove struggle with what I was sure would amount to a righteous hangover.

"You're up early."

I jolted at the sound of Landon's voice, turning quickly to find him standing in the doorway of our bedroom. His hair was mussed and he wore nothing but boxer shorts. Even though he looked a little worse for wear, he was quite the sight to behold.

"Why don't you ever wake up with bedhead?" I complained.

"Just one of those little gifts from the Goddess," Landon replied dryly as he joined me in the kitchen. He planted a kiss on my neck as he leaned around me and snagged a slice of his favorite treat. "What's the special occasion?"

"Why must there be a special occasion?"

"You cooked."

"I made bacon and oatmeal."

"That's still cooking."

"Barely."

"You never cook." Landon moved to the coffee pot and poured himself a mug. "I thought we were going up to the inn for breakfast. I was a little worried when I woke and you were already gone. I thought maybe you'd left without me."

"I wouldn't do that."

Landon arched a dubious eyebrow as he leaned against the

counter. "You would if you thought it would get you out of an argument."

"Are we going to argue?"

"A little bit."

I heaved out a sigh. I knew he wouldn't say "no," yet I was hoping for it all the same. "I thought it would be better to argue here. Clove and Sam stayed at the inn. I'm sure she's hungover. Plus, well, if we fight in front of my family Aunt Tillie will find out what we did last night and she'll be all over that site today."

"Fair enough." Landon sipped and eyed me speculatively. "Do you want to say something?"

"Yes."

"I figured. You can start."

"REO Speedwagon has put out some fine music."

Landon took me by surprise when he chuckled. "Fine. I stand corrected. I promise to dance with you to REO Speedwagon one night this week if you let it go."

That was far too easy. I expected to wear him down with a music argument before we got to the big stuff. "Oh, well ... ."

"I want to talk about you planting the lullaby in my head in the first place," Landon persisted. "I don't like it when you do things like that. You're not supposed to use your magic on me."

"And I don't like using my magic on you. It's just ... this case is different. You can't share information with me. That means I have to use alternative means to get information. I thought it would be easier for you if I slipped out while you slept."

"You thought it would be easier for you," Landon corrected. "You knew I would argue if you told the truth."

"Maybe."

"You're right about this being hard on both of us, Bay," Landon said. "I don't like it any more than you do. We're both trying to do right by each other when it's impossible to tell the truth. I don't expect you to volunteer your plans to me."

"You don't?" That was news to me. "That's not what you said at dinner last night."

"That was wishful thinking, not expectation. I know I can't stop you from chasing this. It's not in your nature to look the other way."

I licked my lips. "It's weird. While I was walking through the woods and trying not to focus on that cougar video that's been making the rounds, I thought about that. About how it would be easier if I could just let it go. It would be the best thing for both of us if I could."

"Not for both of us."

"I didn't want to plant the lullaby," I supplied. "I also didn't want you waking up and wondering where I went. I can't figure out why it didn't work."

"Perhaps it didn't work because your heart wasn't in it."

"Maybe."

"Or perhaps it didn't work because I was only faking being asleep."

I jerked my head in his direction. "You weren't asleep? I assumed you woke up when I left, maybe heard the door shut. Are you saying you weren't asleep in the first place?"

"No. I knew you were going to sneak out."

"How could you possibly know that?"

"Because, while your cousins got so drunk they had to stay at the inn, you nursed the same glass of wine while pretending to refill it," Landon replied, matter-of-fact. "I'm a trained investigator. I watched you. I knew you were going to make a move. Otherwise, you would've had more than one glass of wine."

"I thought you drank more than you obviously did," I admitted ruefully.

"I did the same thing you did. I filled glasses of wine and then gave them to Clove and Thistle."

"Oh." I pursed my lips. "I guess I should have watched you more closely."

"I don't think that's the part of the conversation we need to focus on, Bay," Landon countered. "I'm more interested in the part where you tried to spell me."

"It was for your own good."

"I think you believe that. I'm not sure it's true."

I balked. "It's true. I wanted to make sure you were safe in bed."

"While you were running around the countryside."

"Hey, you wanted to stay out there a lot longer than I did," I argued. "I was ready to come back five minutes after I arrived. You wouldn't have even noticed I was gone if things went according to plan."

"That's the point. What if they hadn't gone according to plan? What if you'd been discovered and taken into custody?"

"Then you would've woken to a very annoying phone call."

"Would I? I'm not so sure. Agent Gibson could've held you for twenty-four hours without allowing you to place a call. Do you think that would've gone over well?"

Huh. That hadn't even occurred to me. "No. I guess not. I didn't think about it."

"I know you didn't." Landon placed his coffee on the counter and moved next to me. "We need new ground rules for this case. Our previous rules are fine for other cases, but this is different."

I was instantly alert. "What kind of ground rules?"

"The type where we both acknowledge we have jobs to do but our relationship is more important," Landon replied without hesitation. "That means if we can't say something, we acknowledge that. But no lies."

"I didn't lie."

"No spells, at least against me. That's not fair."

I blew out a sigh and ran my hand through my damp hair. "Okay. I can live with that. I didn't mean to hurt you."

"You didn't hurt me. I knew what you were doing all along."

"And you followed because you wanted to see for yourself," I mused. "Did you figure out anything last night? I mean ... I know you can't tell me, but I'd feel better knowing that you understand where all of this is going."

"I didn't figure anything out. Gibson is hiding something from me, and I don't like it. I have no idea what he's looking for. It doesn't make any sense."

"Have you noticed there's no wreckage out there?"

"As a matter of fact, I have."

"Was it collected that first night? Was it ever out there?"

"Sweetie, I really don't know. The first day we were there the smoke was too heavy to see anything. Gibson insisted we stay in town yesterday. I assume the wreckage was removed then."

"No, it was gone before I went out there yesterday morning. That means they collected it during the night."

"Which explains why you felt the need to go out there last night."

"I simply wanted to see what they were doing. I'm more confused now than when I left the house."

"Yeah, well, that makes two of us." Landon grabbed a slice of bacon from the plate on the counter and snapped it in half, giving the bigger chunk to me before munching on his portion. "Gibson's full of himself, but he'll have to start talking at some point."

"Why does he outrank you?"

"That's simply part of the game. He's been with the bureau longer, and this is his case. I'm merely auxiliary help."

"Hmm." I bit into the bacon and chewed, thoughtful. "Does the bacon mean you forgive me?"

"I was never really angry. I just wanted to make sure we were on the same page."

"We are. I won't be a butthead again."

"Oh, you'll be a butthead." Landon's eyes twinkled as he grinned. "But you're my butthead. I'm kind of fond of you no matter what you do. No more lullabies, though. I don't like it. It feels ... invasive."

"Even if I pick something like Bob Dylan?"

"No. More. Lullabies."

I held up my hands in capitulation. "Got it. I won't do it again."

"Good." Landon rolled his neck. "Are you really going to make me eat this mush or can we get breakfast in town?"

"Oh, thank the Goddess." I pushed the oatmeal away. "Let's definitely go to town."

"See, we're already back on the right track."

"I can't tell you how relieved I am."

ALIEN INSPIRATION

> Do you think we can order one of those aliens from *Predator* and put it in Margaret Little's house? I'm asking for a friend. Not me. A friend. No, seriously. I'm just asking.
>
> **Aunt Tillie discussing the limitations of online shopping**

TEN

INFINITE SPACE. INFINITE AUNT TILLIE. INFINITE TERROR.

I parked in front of Hypnotic, taking a moment to wave at Landon as he parked across the street. His expression reflected curiosity, but he didn't cross and demand answers. We were trying to compromise. In addition to that, what he didn't say but I picked up was that he figured he was better off not knowing what I was up to.

Oh, sure, he hated being in the dark. As long as he didn't know what I was doing, though, he could honestly deny any allegations Gibson lobbed in my direction without feeling guilty. Landon was an oddly moral man — not that there's anything wrong with that — so he hated lying. I was a witch and sometimes lying came with the job, so I was more flexible. He was right about the lullaby, though. That wasn't fair to him ... although I was considering playing a game that involved all eighties ballads to mess with him. But that would have to wait until this was settled.

"Good morning." I greeted my grumpy-looking cousins much louder than necessary. The way they glared from the center of the room told me they didn't think I was remotely funny. "How is everyone feeling this bright and sunny spring day?"

"Do you want me to come over there and shove something in your mouth?" Thistle challenged. Despite her pink hair, there was nothing genial and frothy about her attitude. "I will. I don't feel well, but I'll totally take the time to wrestle you down and gag you."

"Oh, like you have the strength for that." I flicked her ear as I moved past and flopped on the couch. "So, did both of you get drunk and stay at The Overlook last night, or was that just Clove?"

"It was both of us," Thistle grumbled. "Don't bother making fun of me. I realized my mistake the moment I woke up and found Mom standing at the foot of our bed. She had a tray full of coffee — which I should've liked — but she also had a newspaper article explaining how dyeing your hair can shrivel up your eggs. Apparently, she has grandchildren on the brain."

I snickered. "Nice."

"Yes, well ... ." Thistle shook her head, her gaze murky as she tried to clear the haze from her brain. "Where were you last night, by the way? Why didn't you get drunk and spend the night?"

"Because I'm smarter than you."

"Why really?"

I tugged on my limited patience and barely managed to refrain from snapping at her. "Because I had other things to do ... like sneak out to the scene of the crash and take a look around. The Feds had people out there searching the site again, by the way. They were out there the entire night as far as I can tell."

Thistle's eyes widened. "You went out to the site alone? Are you stupid?"

That was not the reaction I was looking for. "I think you meant to ask if I was brave and awesome."

"No, I meant stupid. Only an idiot would've hiked out there alone in the middle of the night."

"She's right," Clove said, her expression grave. "You could've been eaten by bears ... or fallen and twisted your ankle with no way to contact us ... or kidnapped by Bigfoot."

The disgusted sound mounting in the back of my throat wasn't voluntary. "I wasn't afraid of Bigfoot."

Thistle stared me down. "Oh, please. You might not have been afraid of Bigfoot, but you saw the same video I did about the mountain lion. Sure, it's probably a hoax, but there's no way you could have simply pushed it out of your head."

Crap. I hate that she knows me so well. "I was not afraid of the mountain lion."

"Lies."

"I wasn't."

"More lies."

I shook my head and calmed myself. "If you don't stop saying that, I'll drag you outside and fill your mouth with dirt. How would you like that?"

"It's better than trying to choke down a pack of lies."

"Ugh." I slapped my hand to my forehead and stared at the ceiling. "Why must you always be such a pain?"

"It's genetic." Thistle was unnaturally calm and serious as she regarded me. "You're lucky you weren't caught, Bay. What did Landon say when he realized you'd slipped out and managed to get back without being arrested?"

I shifted on my seat, uncomfortable. "Oh, well, that's the thing." I chewed my bottom lip as I debated how much I should tell them. Ultimately, keeping secrets felt alien (pun intended), so I merely shrugged and barreled forward. "He knew I was going to sneak out, pretended to be asleep and then followed me."

"What?"

I launched into my tale, making sure to keep it short. When I was done, Clove and Thistle were both flabbergasted ... although for entirely different reasons.

"You're lucky he didn't arrest you," Clove said solemnly. "You're also lucky he was there to protect you from Bigfoot."

"I can't believe he doesn't like REO Speedwagon," Thistle complained. "While they're not exactly masterful recording artists, their songs are extremely catchy and great for PMS days. He should be ashamed of his reaction."

I couldn't hide my smirk. "I was thinking the exact same thing. He refuses to back down on REO Speedwagon, though."

"Well, that should make fighting the feeling much easier," Thistle drawled. "Seriously. I kind of want to punch him for making fun of REO Speedwagon. Did you punch him?"

"I fell asleep on his lap."

Thistle's eyebrows shot up. "Seriously? Good grief. Only you would fall asleep while spying on the government. What is wrong with you? You're like the worst Mulder ever."

Clove furrowed her brow. "What's a Mulder?"

"Fox Mulder," Thistle automatically answered. "From *The X-Files*."

"Oh, right." Clove made a face. "You know I don't like science fiction television shows. I'm much more into home renovation shows. I prefer learning something from television."

Now it was my turn to roll my eyes. "You like watching those *Real Housewives of Whatever Bar is Open Tonight* and you know it. You don't watch home renovation shows."

Clove folded her arms over her chest. "I could watch those shows."

"But you don't." I shifted my eyes to Thistle. "Landon swears up and down that nothing else happened after I fell asleep. He says the Feds simply walked back and forth across the field."

"They're looking for something." All traces of a hangover were devoid from Thistle's face as she rubbed the back of her neck. "That drone must have had something important on it."

"Ah. So now you admit it's a drone." I felt vindicated.

"I guess it could be a plane, but I think we would've heard about a missing plane at this point," Thistle countered. "And the third alternative —the one in which aliens are running around the countryside — will give me nightmares. I mean ... what if you'd run into an alien in the woods last night?"

"I would've hoped for E.T."

"I know you're joking to cover for the fact that you're relieved Landon didn't melt down and have some righteous hissy fit about what you were doing, but is anyone else worried that he doesn't know what's going on? He's not really lying to you. That Gibson guy is lying to him."

I hadn't really looked at it from that perspective before. "You're right. He was fascinated to watch them search last night. I think he was happy to let me sneak out because it gave him an excuse to follow."

"And you said you're not fighting," Clove pointed out. "That's a bonus."

"Yeah. I wouldn't be happy if we were fighting." I scratched the side of my nose, debating. "I don't know where to look next. I can go back to the scene, cut across Hollow Creek, but I'm not sure there's anything left to see out there if I can't get closer."

"Well, lucky for you I have an idea on that front," Thistle said, leaning forward so she could snag the laptop sitting on the coffee table. "My father happened to email this morning. He's fishing for a visit. What's interesting about his message is that he mentioned a group of people checking into the Dragonfly last night."

The Dragonfly was the competing inn my father and uncles had opened. Initially, I worried their return to Hemlock Cove would cause problems, but it hadn't been nearly as bad as I envisioned. "Okay, I'll bite," I said after a beat. "Who is staying at the Dragonfly?"

"A group of bloggers."

"I don't know why that should excite me."

"They're alien bloggers," Clove supplied. "We were looking them up right before you arrived."

"Here is their site." Thistle turned her laptop so I could see the screen.

"Aliens are among us." I read aloud as I studied the web page. "You're basically saying these guys believe all the alien abduction nonsense. How is this helpful?"

"They're staying at the Dragonfly ... and they're a lot more knowledgeable than us."

"They probably have hats made out of tinfoil," I argued. "They're not going to be able to help."

"Do you have another place to look?"

Ugh. I hated it when she had a point. "Fine." I blew out a sigh. "But if they're weird, I'm blaming you."

"I'd expect nothing less."

CLOVE AND THISTLE closed Hypnotic so they could ride out to the Dragonfly with me. It was a slow day and their hangovers required nursing, which would happen when our fathers opted to spoil them with food and drink. Plus, they didn't want to be left out of the fun. Even though they thought I was an idiot for taking off into the woods on my own the night before, I could tell they were both disappointed to have missed out on the adventure. I would tell the story for years to come, and they would always be the losers who got so drunk they had to stay at the inn and only make cameos at the start of the tale.

My father was in the lobby when we entered. He stood behind the main desk and widened his eyes when he saw us. "You guys aren't running from the law, are you?"

"Ha, ha." I gave him a hug. Our relationship wasn't exactly easy — I was frustrated that he moved away when I was a kid and I couldn't quite get over it, although I was trying — but we were making progress. "How are things out here?"

"They're fine." My father wasn't an idiot. He recognized we rarely stopped by for a genuine visit. We almost always had an agenda. Now that I think about it, that wasn't very nice. We should probably stop by without an agenda once or twice. I would have to make a mental note of it, which technically turned the visit into something with an agenda, but I couldn't think too long on that without making my head explode.

"How are things with you, Bay?" Dad's gaze was pointed.

"They're fine, too. It's been fairly quiet at the inn. Clove and Thistle got drunk and stayed there last night, but I was a good girl and didn't over imbibe."

Thistle scorched me with a hateful look. "Don't even start."

Dad chuckled. He was used to our antics. "We're between tours. I don't see any problem with having a drink or two ... or ten ... as long as you're not driving. How are things at the guesthouse? Are you and Landon settling in together relatively well?"

Landon was another sore spot with my father. When he left Hemlock Cove, I was a child. He saw me sporadically through the years after that, but never for more than a day or two in a row. When he returned full time, I was an adult with a boyfriend. He couldn't quite seem to wrap his head around it, especially because Landon refused to hold back when he felt my father was out of line.

"Things are good in the guesthouse." I refused to lie. "It's an adjustment, but it's not really the adjustment I thought it would be. Landon was practically living there on weekends anyway. He had to go back to Traverse City three nights a week, but he worked hard to cut that to two nights. Otherwise, he was with me whenever he could arrange it. It's really not that different."

"I understand that, but you had Thistle and Clove there, too," Dad pointed out. "Six people living together — which is how it must have felt when everyone had overnight guests — is much different than two people living together."

He wasn't wrong. "It's honestly been fine. Nice even. Knowing Landon doesn't have to pack up on Monday mornings is a relief. He still has work, of course, but that's his home now. It makes everyone more relaxed."

"I'm glad." Dad looked as if he meant it. "So ... why are you guys out here in the middle of the day?"

His tone caused me to balk. "Maybe we just wanted to see you guys. Have you ever considered that?"

"No." Dad shook his head, firm. "You just told me that Clove and Thistle are both hungover, which means driving out here wasn't something they'd planned to do. That means you're out here for a reason. We only have one group of guests, and I happen to know that Teddy messaged Thistle about those guests earlier today. I can put two and two together."

Crud on a cracker. I hate getting pegged by my father ... especially when I'm guilty. "Oh, well ... ."

"We want to talk to the alien dudes," Thistle admitted, ignoring the glare I lobbed in her direction. "There's something weird going on at the crash site and there's an out-of-town FBI agent in charge of everything, and he's already threatened us with jail time. We don't know where else to look."

"Okay, but just for the record, you don't actually think there are aliens running around, do you?" Dad looked legitimately worried.

"Of course not," I scoffed.

"Good."

"Aliens are third on our list."

"And if they are aliens, we've narrowed them to the ones from *Invasion of the Body Snatchers*," Clove offered helpfully. "Mrs. Little was out there the first day and she's acting weird. It's either aliens or she's messing with Aunt Tillie. We're fifty-fifty on it right now."

Dad's mouth dropped open. "You cannot be serious."

"Why not?" I challenged. "I think it's a drone. I think it was some experimental thing that the public isn't supposed to know about and that's why they're being so secretive."

"Sounds logical," Dad noted. "Maybe they had some sort of proprietary technology on there that they don't want anyone to stumble across."

"That's possible," I agreed. "It also could be aliens." I surprised myself with the admission. Sure, I initially said it because I knew it would throw my father for a loop. I wasn't above messing with him. The sad truth was, though, that I wasn't as reticent to the possibility as I should've been. I thought Clove was an idiot for buying into Aunt Tillie's hype, but it turned out I wasn't ready to completely turn my back on the idea.

"You guys are messing with me, right?" Dad looked legitimately worried. "There's no way you believe it's aliens. This is simply one of those bits you do when you're looking for attention."

Thistle drew her eyebrows together. "We don't do bits."

"Sure you do. What do you think all that 'you're dead to me' and 'I'm going to make you eat dirt' stuff is?"

"Um ... that's the way we roll."

"They're bits," Dad challenged. "You guys don't really mean them. They're simply part of the Winchester charm."

"Well, I hate to burst your bubble, but we mean the dirt thing," I argued. "I've shoved dirt in Thistle's mouth at least five times."

"When you were kids."

"No, about a year and a half ago I shoved snow in her mouth. It was dirty snow, so that counts."

"I remember that." Thistle's expression turned dark. "I haven't paid you back for that yet. Thanks for reminding me."

"No problem."

Dad shook his head. "See, I think this is part of the act, too. There's no sense in arguing about it. You won't admit what you're doing."

"Probably not," I agreed, leaning against the counter. "With that in mind, I know you asked what we're doing here. I was kind of hoping we could all have lunch together."

"You guys, me, Teddy and Warren?"

"And whatever guests you have handy on the premises." I was trying to be nonchalant, but I didn't think I had the talent to carry it off.

"That's what I figured," Dad said dryly, shaking his head. "We're having French Dip sandwiches and fries. How does that sound?"

"Like the best hangover food ever." Thistle brightened considerably. "Did I mention how glad I am that we decided to come and visit you guys out of the blue with no ulterior motives?"

Dad merely shook his head as he regarded her. "This is getting easier for everyone, isn't it? At least you guys are comfortable lying to us without feeling guilty. That's progress."

I bobbed my head. "That's exactly what I was thinking."

ALIEN INSPIRATION

" There was a time I thought your mother was pregnant with an alien, Thistle. It turns out that pain in the ass she had was simply prophetic. You're not half-alien. You're all jerk.

Aunt Tillie tells Thistle how it is

ELEVEN

ONE WITCH SAW IT COMING.

We chatted with our fathers for an hour, but my eyes were constantly on the stairs. Most of the conversation revolved around mundane issues like Thistle's naked statue, which made her father uncomfortable. Clove talked about how she was gearing up to work on the gardens at the Dandridge, the lighthouse she lived in with Sam. I refrained from bringing up aliens again, even though they were obviously the elephant in the room.

"Don't worry, Bay," Dad said finally as he topped off my iced tea. "I know they're coming down for lunch. They told us that yesterday. They're going out after that."

I adopted an air of innocence. "I wasn't thinking about that."

"Uh-huh." Dad wasn't convinced. "What were you thinking about?"

"How nice it is to spend time with you."

"You're a rotten liar."

"That's not true. Aunt Tillie conducted classes on lying when we were teenagers. I was her star pupil."

Thistle cleared her throat. "I was her star pupil."

"You're both crackheads," Clove corrected. "I was her star pupil."

"Just what every father wants to hear," Warren drawled. Clove's father was used to being manipulated, but even he looked unhappy with the conversation. "Tell us about this new FBI agent. What's his deal?"

"He's a douche," I answered automatically.

"Tell us how you really feel," Dad said, smirking.

"That is how I really feel."

"Are you sure you're not just saying that because Landon dislikes him?"

"There's no doubt Landon hates him," I agreed. "That doesn't mean he's not a douche."

"He threatened to arrest us the day of the crash," Thistle explained. "He also has the woods surrounding Potter's Field closed off. We can't get out there, but Bay and Landon managed to get fairly close last night."

My father's expressive face couldn't mask his surprise. "Wait ... you and Landon snuck out there together? Isn't he part of the investigation?"

"Yes and no," I hedged. "Agent Gibson is keeping him out of the loop. Landon has orders to follow, but he's not happy about it."

"Probably because he doesn't like keeping anything from you."

"That's part of it," I agreed. "The other part is that he's used to being in charge and doesn't take kindly to others ordering him around."

"He likes it when Bay orders him around," Thistle corrected. "She has to wear black leather and carry a whip when she does it."

As usual, Thistle didn't realize she took it a step too far until my father started coughing into his hand, his cheeks turning a bright red.

"Nice." I glared daggers at Thistle. "Why can't you ever think before you speak?"

Thistle shrugged. "It's a family thing. Even I'm not strong enough to break our genetic code. You know that."

"Whatever."

"Hey, don't blame me for this." Thistle's temper ratcheted up a notch. "Aunt Tillie made me this way. It's on her."

As if on cue, Aunt Tillie picked that moment to pop up in the small sitting room off the lobby. She didn't look out of place — even though our fathers pretty much loathed her — and she didn't seem surprised to find us hanging out in a different inn.

"Did someone just say my name?"

Dad moved to stand and then sat again, dumbfounded. "When did you get here?"

Aunt Tillie shrugged. "I don't know. Thirty minutes ago or so. I was in the lobby going through your books. You should charge a cleaning fee. All the other inns in the area do it. You're leaving money on the table."

Dad turned a set of incredulous eyes to me. "She went through our books?"

I sensed danger, but there wasn't much I could do about it. Trying to control Aunt Tillie was like herding cats inside a room made of tuna. "She's not wrong about the cleaning fee. That's the way we do it at The Overlook."

Dad pressed the tip of his tongue to his top lip as he collected himself. "I see."

"I've been looking all over for you three." Aunt Tillie shifted her attention to me, ignoring the obvious fury pooling around my father. "We need to talk about strategy."

That sounded like a terrible idea.

"Why would we want to strategize with you?" Thistle challenged, taking the words out of my mouth. "If we team up with you, we'll end up in jail."

"Whatever, mouth." Aunt Tillie flicked Thistle's ear before grabbing an extra chair from next to the wall and pushing it between Warren and me. She didn't bother asking if she could join us, instead simply forcing the situation, which was her way. "We need to talk about what we're going to do."

"I'm almost afraid to ask," Teddy said nervously. "What do you want them to do?"

"Help me find the aliens, of course," Aunt Tillie replied without hesitation. "I can't do it without a little bit of help, even though that's hard to admit. There's too much ground to cover."

AMANDA M. LEE

I didn't miss the weighted look Teddy shot my father. "Aliens?"

"Just ignore her." Dad made a dismissive motion with his hand. "It's some new bit they've developed."

I found my anger building. "We don't do bits."

"Absolutely not," Aunt Tillie agreed, grabbing an empty teacup from the center of the table. "Everything we do is deathly serious. The fate of the world often lies in our hands, so we can't waste time doing bits."

"Oh, well, that's not dramatic or anything." Thistle rolled her eyes. "Speaking of the aliens, though, we're still leaning toward the drone theory."

"Maybe, but you're warming to the alien idea," Aunt Tillie countered. "I know you guys. You haven't been able to get it out of your heads. That's why you're here."

"And why are we here?" I asked, playing for time. Admitting Aunt Tillie was right seemed a bad idea, which meant I had to find a way to shut her down before she embarrassed us.

"You're here because that group of alien investigators is here," Aunt Tillie replied, matter-of-fact. "They're here because they understand the sort of situation we're dealing with."

Teddy leaned forward to stare directly into Aunt Tillie's eyes. "And what situation is that?"

"We have an *Invasion of the Body Snatchers* situation," Aunt Tillie explained. "To be precise, that's a long title. I was thinking of switching it to *The Faculty*. That's much more streamlined and basically the same story."

I pressed the heel of my hand to my forehead. "I think they get the general gist."

"Speak for yourself," Dad challenged. "I don't understand any of this. I'm particularly confused about the part where you guys are talking about aliens as if they're real."

Aunt Tillie's glare was withering. "Of course they're real, Jack. Aliens have been among us for years. How else do you explain the Kardashians? Oh, and the Baldwins. Oh, and all those people on those home renovation shows Clove insists on watching."

Now it was my turn to be confused. "You think the home renovation people are aliens?"

"Who else would build a fireplace out of pipe cleaners?"

"I'm pretty sure that never happened," Clove said.

"Of course it did. Would I make something like that up?"

"Yes," Clove, Thistle and I answered in unison.

"Pfft." Aunt Tillie rolled her eyes. "I'm telling you, aliens are real and the invasion is finally happening. What do you think I've been doing the last few days? I'm tracking their movements."

That sounded unlikely. Sure, it was possible Aunt Tillie got out a map and circled areas on it. Tracking actual aliens, though, was something else entirely.

"And what did you find while tracking them?" Warren asked finally.

"They're taking over the area." Aunt Tillie was grim. "We're going to need help to end this here. Hemlock Cove is ground zero. We can't let it spread."

Dad sipped his coffee for a beat before sliding his eyes to me. "Have I mentioned I love your visits? We really should do this more often."

I grinned. "You knew stuff like this was going to happen when you moved back. You can't blame us."

"Oh, I can blame you. This is ... unbelievable."

"Just wait until Aunt Tillie meets your guests," Thistle interjected. "It's only going to get worse."

"That's what I'm afraid of."

THE ALIEN HUNTERS TURNED out to be a trio of men — maybe teenagers, they looked young enough — wearing expensive boots, cargo pants and heavy flannel shirts. One of them had long hair; the other two boasted enough product to make eighties mousse fans jealous.

"This is Morgan Johnson, Ryan Blake and Jace Penfield." Dad's smile was tight as he made introductions around the dining room table. "Gentlemen, these are our daughters Bay, Clove and Thistle."

The men, who were definitely younger than us, brightened considerably as they sat at the table.

"It's nice to make your acquaintance." Jace sat next to me and extended his hand. "We had no idea that the Dragonfly boasted such lovely accessories."

The statement was odd ... in more ways than one. "Thank you." I briefly shook Jace's hand before Aunt Tillie barreled between us and took the chair Jace was selecting.

"I'm Tillie Winchester," she announced, grabbing a sandwich from the middle of the table. "I'll be leading the group today."

I watched as Jace curiously eyed Aunt Tillie. "I'm sorry, but ... what?"

"I'll be leading the group," Aunt Tillie repeated as she kicked my calf under the table. "I can't reach the au jus sauce. I need some."

I could've told her to figure a way to get the dipping sauce herself, but that seemed like a recipe for disaster. "Hold on." I leaned over and ladled some of the brown juice into a small bowl. "Is that enough?"

"For now." Aunt Tillie immediately dipped her sandwich into the juice before continuing. "I think we should eat and then get going. We're going to lose the light if we're not careful. It's spring, but Daylight Savings doesn't arrive until next weekend, so it still gets dark early."

I had to give him credit. Jace was obviously confused by Aunt Tillie's bossy nature, but he didn't react out of anger or annoyance. "You want to go with us while we conduct our initial search?" he asked finally.

"No, I want to take you with us while we conduct our third search," Aunt Tillie corrected. "We're ahead of you on this one. You should be happy to have our expertise."

"Um ... ." Jace looked to me for help.

"We saw your blog thing on the internet," I explained, hoping to steer the conversation to a safer topic. "You wrote that you were staying at the Dragonfly. That was convenient because our fathers own it. We've been investigating the scene of the crash a bit, too."

"It's my understanding that the FBI is keeping the site closed off," Morgan interjected. He wore wire-rimmed glasses that made him look smart, which seemed to be exactly what he was going for. "We were told we wouldn't be able to get close to the site."

"It's not easy," I agreed, "but it's not impossible. They've been conducting grid searches day and night. We can't get to the exact spot. We can get close enough to hide in the woods and watch them."

"Really?" Morgan was understandably intrigued. "You've made it out there to spy?"

I nodded. "Twice. I went yesterday morning and then again in the middle of the night."

Dad's eyes flashed. "You walked through the woods in the middle of the night? Are you crazy?"

I was getting sick and tired of hearing that question. "I don't think 'crazy' is the appropriate word."

"What word would you use?" Dad didn't back down. "I know that Clove and Thistle were drunk last night. You told me that. That means you went by yourself."

"Not exactly." I squirmed in my seat. "My roommate went with me. I believe I mentioned that earlier. You must have missed that part."

Dad scrubbed at his forehead. "Your roommate. You mean ... ." He caught on at the exact right moment and refrained from saying Landon's name. It wasn't that I thought the alien hunters were bad guys — or likely to cause trouble, for that matter — but I didn't want to put Landon's job on the line. If word got out that he was sneaking through the woods with me to spy on his own people, it wouldn't end well.

"It doesn't matter." I was firm as I doused my fries with ketchup. "I wasn't alone. That's the important thing."

"I guess." Dad didn't look convinced, but he wisely dropped the subject.

"What did you see out there?" Ryan asked. "I mean ... if they were working in the middle of the night, they must have been doing something important."

I shrugged, noncommittal. "I don't know what they were doing. It didn't look different from what I saw them doing in the afternoon. They were conducting grid searches."

"I'm not familiar with grid searches," Teddy interjected. "What are they?"

"It's when you take a group of people and space them several feet apart," I explained. "They were all dressed in protective clothing and staring at the ground. I have no idea what they were looking for. They didn't find it during the day, though, which is why the search continued into the night."

"What about wreckage?" Morgan pulled a small notebook from his pocket and started jotting notes. "What did the wreckage look like?"

"I never saw any wreckage."

"But ... how is that possible?"

"The day of the crash, the smoke was unbelievable," I explained, looking to Thistle and Clove for help. "Tell them."

"She's right," Clove volunteered. "You couldn't see anything but black smoke for miles. It was too thick to see what actually crashed."

"And then the Feds showed up and ordered us away," Thistle added. "They cleared out the area quickly. They even shut down the highway on the far side to make sure people didn't get close enough to see anything."

"They reacted fast," Jace mused. "That doesn't surprise me, but how they knew where the crash would occur is fairly mind-boggling. They must have been tracking the vessel."

"The space vessel?" Dad asked, disdain evident.

Clearly used to nonbelievers, Jace merely shrugged. "Yes."

"What about when you went back to the scene?" Morgan prodded. "It's my understanding that agents were positioned so no one could approach."

"That's true, but I'm more familiar with the area, so I knew a way to get near the property," I explained. "I'm sure they thought the water would serve as a barrier, but I know a way across the water that's largely hidden."

"Really?" Morgan's eyes flashed with delight. "Could you show us?"

"Maybe." I glanced between faces. "What will you do if I get you out there?"

"We have equipment," Jace replied. "We can scan for radioactivity. We also know the sort of tracks to look for."

"Alien tracks?" Dad challenged. "Are you saying you've seen alien footprints before?"

"We have." Jace refused to rise to Dad's rather obvious bait. "If something is out there, we'll be able to find proof quickly."

"You can't get too close to the site," I warned. "They'll see you. I can get you into the woods near the site. If you have the right equipment — maybe binoculars or something — you'll have a better chance at seeing what they're up to."

"We have all of that." Jace's smile was sweet ... and maybe a bit flirty. I couldn't be sure because he was so much younger than me. "It seems this was a lucky meeting of the minds."

"That's exactly what I said." Aunt Tillie had finished her sandwich. Juice dripped from her chin. "If you guys had listened to me fifteen minutes ago, we'd already be on our way."

Ryan's expression was dubious when it landed on Aunt Tillie. "Ma'am, are you sure you want to come with us? The woods are dangerous and you're ... old."

Aunt Tillie narrowed her eyes to dangerous slits. "Who are you calling old?"

Uh-oh. I rested a hand on Aunt Tillie's forearm to get her attention. "I think everyone is old to them." I kept my voice low. "I'm sure they think I'm old, too."

"You are old," Aunt Tillie shot back. "I'm in my prime."

"Just ... don't alienate them. They might be able to help us."

"Fine." Aunt Tillie rolled her eyes. "But if they keep calling me old I'll curse their balls to turn blue and shrivel up. Then we'll see who's old."

"Yes, well, that sounds delightful." I rolled my neck and cringed when I found Dad staring at me. "What? Everything will be fine. You have nothing to worry about."

"I don't want you to go," Dad said. "I think it's a mistake."

"Well, you can't stop us."

"And what if I call Chief Terry and Landon? Will that stop you?"

Wait ... was he threatening me? "I can't believe you just said that."

Dad refused to back down. "I'll do what it takes to protect you. This is a terrible idea."

I spoke before I thought better of it. "That's something Mom would do."

Dad's eyes filled with fire. "That won't stop me from calling Chief Terry. I'll do what I think is right."

"Well, great," Aunt Tillie drawled. "You've turned into a tattletale, Jack. I hope you're proud of yourself."

"Wipe your mouth, Tillie," Dad barked, handing her a napkin. "You've got food all down the front of your shirt."

"That's natural camouflage for the woods." Aunt Tillie tapped the side of her head. "I'm always thinking. You should try it."

Dad didn't bother to hide his glare. "I'm calling Chief Terry."

"Fine." I was resigned. "That still won't stop us."

"We'll just see about that."

ALIEN INSPIRATION

> Why would aliens come here to probe people? Seriously, you travel light years to find another planet and race, and the first thing you do is shove a doodad up their ... well, you know. That makes zero sense. I think *The X-Files* had it wrong.
>
> **Bay trying to make sense of a movie**

TWELVE

SHE DIDN'T FIND HER DREAMS ... HER DREAMS FOUND HER.

We took two vehicles to Hollow Creek, the alien hunters following us. When we parked, they seemed confused.

"I don't understand." Morgan shifted his pack as he glanced at the murky water. "Isn't the field that way?" He pointed for emphasis. "How are we supposed to get across the water? Do you expect us to swim?"

"No." I fobbed my car to lock it, although it seemed unnecessary given our location. "We're going to walk across the water."

"Walk?" Jace appeared at my elbow, his smile even flirtier than when I last saw him at the Dragonfly. He was starting to make me uncomfortable. "Are you telling me you can walk on water? I'm not saying I doubt you or anything. I guess if anyone could do it, it would be you."

Oh, geez. I could feel Thistle's eyes on me — and I already knew the expression I would see there should I look — so I remained focused on the water. "It's an optical illusion. There are spots so shallow you can walk across. You just have to know the trail."

"And you know the trail?" Ryan queried.

"I do." I bent over and untied my shoes. "Your feet will still get wet, so I suggest taking off your shoes."

"These boots are waterproof." Jace winked. "They're specially made and everything."

"They look like normal combat boots," Thistle argued.

"Well, they're not." Jace wasn't nearly as enamored with Thistle as he was with me. "We'll be fine. Treks like this are exactly why we bought these boots."

"Knock yourself out." I helped Aunt Tillie remove her boots after finishing with my sneakers. "I have a towel." I held it up for emphasis. "The water is cold, but it doesn't take long. We'll dry our feet on the other side."

"Is that what you did yesterday?" Clove asked.

"Yeah. It's a well-honed system now."

"We should've just bought waterproof boots," Thistle groused.

"Well, it's too late for that."

I took the lead, which didn't sit well with Aunt Tillie, but given her age, Thistle and I silently came to a meeting of the minds in which we forced her to walk between us. It took only three minutes to pick our way through the shallow spots, and once on the other side, Jace was appropriately impressed.

"How did you guys figure that out?"

"We've been forced to visit this place on occasion for other stories," I replied, drying Aunt Tillie's feet first. I dosed them with a bit of warming magic when the guys weren't looking, and she seemed none the worse for wear when pulling on her boots.

Once Thistle, Clove and I were settled, I pointed toward the trees. "We have to walk through there a bit. I didn't see an agent when I was here yesterday, but that doesn't mean they haven't branched out. Keep a close watch. Whatever you do, don't walk completely out of the trees when we get to the field. They'll be able to see you if you do."

Jace mock saluted. "No problem. You've already proven your worth to this team. We'll totally listen to whatever you have to say."

"Great," I said dryly, shaking my head as Thistle moved to my side.

"Someone has a crush on you," she sang under her breath.

"He does not. He's like ... fifteen."

"I asked when they were packing to leave at the Dragonfly," Thistle countered. "They're all nineteen. Ryan made sure to tell me they were adults ... and mature ones at that."

"Nineteen?" I felt sick to my stomach. "They're children."

"They're children with equipment we need." Thistle sobered. "Plus, if the Feds catch wind we're out here we can always sacrifice the kids during our escape."

That sounded mean ... and kind of brilliant. "I don't know if I'm comfortable with that," I hedged.

"Fine. Go to jail. I'll abandon you, too."

I scowled. "You're a true joy. Has anyone ever told you that?"

"I tell myself that every day. I don't care what you say. I'm not going to jail, and if we have to sacrifice these idiots to save ourselves I'm fine with it."

"At least you're finally embracing the lessons I taught you when you were younger," Aunt Tillie announced, pushing through Thistle and me to take the lead. "Better late than never, huh?"

Thistle didn't take the comment as a compliment. "I'll abandon you, too, old lady."

"You won't get the chance because I'll be sacrificing you," Aunt Tillie shot back. "Now ... keep up. I'm dying to see what they're doing out here. I bet it's diabolical. In fact, I bet they've already taken some of the aliens into custody and they're looking for the ones that got away."

"I thought it was like *Invasion of the Body Snatchers*," I challenged. "That means the aliens are like worms ... or goo ... and manage to hop into people to take them over. How is it possible the government took goo into custody?"

"I don't know." Aunt Tillie's irritation was on full display. "Do I look like I'm up on the latest government containment facilities? I just know they did it."

"Fine." I held up my hands. I was starting to feel foolish regarding the whole alien thing. I wanted to go back to my drone hunch, but we were already out here, so it seemed unwise to voice that opinion. "Let's see if we can find some aliens, shall we?"

"The odds of us actually finding aliens is three-thousand-to-one," Morgan interjected imperiously. "Either the federal government has already destroyed them or they're long gone. We might find tracks, though."

"And what good will tracks do us?" Thistle challenged.

"It will prove we're not alone."

"Uh-huh." Thistle flicked her eyes to me. "We should have brought Reese's Pieces with us. We could have left a trail that leads back to Hollow Creek and camped there until they found us."

"Next time." I grinned because I knew it would irritate her. "Now, cut the chatter. We're getting close to the tree line."

"Yes, ma'am." Jace winked. "I'll stick close to you to make sure you're protected. I mean ... if you want."

Crappity crap crap. "Maybe later."

"I'll stick close anyway."

"Great."

EVERYONE WAS SILENT WHEN we hit the edge of the trees. Jace, Morgan and Ryan immediately started hunting through their packs to retrieve items — most of which I didn't recognize — while Thistle, Clove, Aunt Tillie and I crouched behind some heavy foliage and stared at the field.

"It doesn't look too busy," Clove said finally, her voice low. "Maybe they've found everything they're looking for and are packing up."

"Maybe." I squinted so I could see the vehicles parked on the far side of the field. "There're only three trucks over there. There were at least twenty vehicles parked there yesterday, and a good ten or so last night."

"So maybe Clove is right," Thistle suggested. "Maybe they're finished. Maybe they found what they were looking for."

"Or simply gave up." I tilted my head to the side, considering. "The thing is, the way they were searching the grid makes me think they were looking for something small."

"You mean it wasn't an alien." Thistle's grin was quick. "Maybe it was something on the ship itself."

"Drone," I automatically corrected. "I'm back to thinking it was a drone."

"Then you're stupid." Aunt Tillie cuffed the back of my head, causing me to shrink away from her. "It was a ship. It wasn't a drone."

"You don't know that," I grumbled, rubbing my head. "No one saw what crashed."

"That's because it was an alien ship with a cloaking device," Aunt Tillie explained. "It was invisible. The cloaking device remained intact upon impact, and that's why we only saw smoke."

"A cloaking device? Like on *Star Trek*?"

"Better than that." Aunt Tillie made a face. "I mean ... you saw that movie with the whales, right? They landed right in the middle of the park and there was a huge depression in the ground. How did someone not walk into that thing and alert the authorities there was a huge invisible ship in the park?"

"They had their sensors trained on the area and knew when people approached." I had no idea why I was arguing the point ... other than my *Star Trek* love manifested in such a way I had no choice but to stand up for one of the better movies. "It's totally possible."

"And people say I'm nutty," Aunt Tillie grumbled. "The simple fact of the matter is my theory makes the most sense."

"I think Bay's theory makes more sense," Thistle challenged. "The reason the FBI knew to converge on the area so quickly is because the drone belonged to them. They were ready because they knew exactly where it went down."

"No."

Clove wasn't in the mood to engage in an argument. "Can we just let it go? What does it matter?"

I ignored the question. "Maybe it wasn't an aircraft crash," I suggested. "Maybe it was a tactical vehicle or something and suffered mechanical failure."

"No. It was definitely a crash." Aunt Tillie was having none of it. "Don't be a dunce. I'm right and you know it."

"Just saying you're right doesn't make you right."

Aunt Tillie snorted. "Of course it does. Are you new? You learned this particular lesson when you were three. I'm always right."

"Yeah, yeah." I shook my head and stared to the east, my eyes lighting when I caught a flash of color that didn't belong in the environment. "Isn't that Hank's house over there?"

Aunt Tillie nodded without turning to see what I was pointing at. "Yeah. He lives really close to the site. I don't think that's a coincidence."

"Because the aliens were coming to visit him?" Thistle asked sarcastically.

"Go ahead and laugh. Hank has been visited multiple times. The aliens want to share knowledge with him."

That made absolutely no sense. "What knowledge? The guy lives in the woods by himself. He doesn't have indoor plumbing, which means he craps in the woods. What could the aliens possibly learn from him?"

"How to survive."

"Whatever." I slapped at my arm when I felt something bite into my flesh. Bug season was gearing up, and one of my greatest fears was getting Lyme disease. It was too early in the season for that. "Maybe we should pay Hank a visit to see if he knows something. He's been out here from the beginning."

"That's not a bad idea." Thistle watched our idiot alien hunters use a tape measure to gauge the length of something they found on the ground. "What are you guys doing?"

"Trying to ascertain if this is an alien footprint," Jace answered. "We're seventy-five percent sure it is."

I moved to where they stood and frowned at what they considered a print. "That's a hole in the ground."

"It's a footprint."

"I think it used to be some sort of nest."

"It's a footprint."

I pictured myself banging my head against a brick wall and abandoned the argument. "We're heading over there. A guy we know lives in that house. If you want to come, you can. If not, we'll swing by on our way back."

Jace straightened his neck, his attention shifting quickly. "Someone lives out here?"

"Yeah. He's a local … guy." I was about to say "kook" but thought better of it. Jace and his friends were kooks. "He lives right over there. We figure it can't hurt to visit him."

"Definitely. I'll go with you."

"To protect me?"

"To protect the world."

"Right." I was starting to feel old ... and ridiculous. "Well, come on. I doubt Hank will be happy to see us, but it can't hurt to see what he's up to."

HANK WAS DEFINITELY not happy to see us.

"Get off my property or I'll start shooting!"

I couldn't see him, but the way his voice carried told me he was in the barn. Jace, Morgan and Ryan immediately dropped to the ground and covered their heads, whispering what sounded like a prayer amongst themselves. The rest of us remained standing. This was hardly the first warning we'd gotten in the woods.

"It's me, Hank," Aunt Tillie called out, unperturbed. "We were checking out the crash site and then realized we were close to your place, so we came over to have a quick chat. You don't have to worry about us trying to take over your property."

Hank poked his head out of the barn. The door was nearly closed. I couldn't see the gun he threatened to shoot us with, but I had no doubt he was armed. From what I could tell the guy was always carrying.

"Tillie?"

Aunt Tillie nodded. "Yeah, it's us."

Hank stepped through the opening, a rifle clutched in his hands.

He didn't point it at us, but he didn't point it downward either. I had a feeling this wasn't exactly going to be a warm welcome. "You're supposed to whistle before you visit."

I stilled. Whistle?

"I forgot my whistle," Aunt Tillie responded, blasé. "I wasn't planning on stopping by. I didn't realize how close your place was to where we were headed. I wanted to touch base."

Hank didn't move from his spot in front of the barn. It almost seemed like he was trying to cut us off should we try to enter the structure. "You still should've whistled."

"I will. Next time."

Something occurred to me. "Is he the reason you always carry a whistle when you're going hunting?"

"No. I carry the whistle because I like to scare people with loud noises. I have a special whistle for Hank. It sounds like a pretty flute."

"Awesome." Thistle made an exaggerated face. "Can you ask your buddy about what he's witnessed out here? This place gives me the creeps."

She wasn't the only one. The house was so ramshackle it reminded me of something straight out of a horror movie. It looked like something a down-on-their-luck family would move into because they had nowhere else to go. That was before the murderous ghosts arrived, of course, and things turned bloody.

"Calm down," Aunt Tillie ordered. "I've got everything under control. Hank is a good guy. There's no need to be worried."

"Then ask him," Thistle pressed.

Aunt Tillie raised her hands and took a deliberate step forward. "We come in peace."

Thistle flicked her eyes to me. "Is she kidding?"

I shrugged, unsure.

"I know you come in peace, Tillie." Hank's agitation was evident. "Now isn't a good time. I've got a lot to do. It's spring, and you know what that means."

"What does that mean?" Clove asked.

"The power grid is more likely to go in warm weather," Aunt Tillie explained. "That way 'The Man' can blame it on a storm. Hank has to be ready, because if the power grid goes, the end of the world will officially be upon us."

Oh, good grief. I could only take so much. "Hank, we don't want to take up much of your time," I interjected. "We just want to know if you've seen anything in Potter's Field. We know the Feds have been searching for three days. They've been doing it at night, too. They're close. You must have been watching their progress."

"They're lying," Hank said. "They said nothing crashed, but I know that's not true. They tried to get me to leave my house, but I refused."

"Did they say why they wanted you to leave?" I asked.

"Just that it was national security. I have no intention of leaving. This is my home. They'll have to kill me to get me off this land."

"I'm sure they don't want that."

"Oh, really?" Hank turned sarcastic. "Have you heard of Ruby Ridge? What about Waco?"

The last thing we needed was to go off on a tangent. "They won't come after you. I'm sure of it." My curiosity hopped when a noise emanated from the barn, a high-pitched warning that almost sounded like a growl. It was loud enough that Hank jerked his head to stare inside. "Do you have animals out here?"

"What?" Hank forced himself to focus on me. "No. I don't have animals. Animals won't survive the apocalypse."

"Okay, well ... what's in the barn?"

"Nothing." Hank straightened. "Why do you think something is in the barn?"

Was he kidding? "I heard something in there."

"You're imagining things."

I turned to Aunt Tillie for help. "You heard it, right?"

Aunt Tillie's expression was thoughtful. Finally, she shook her head. "I didn't hear anything."

"But ... ."

She cut me off with a firm headshake. "I didn't hear anything, Bay." Her tone warned there would be retribution if I pushed further. "We should be going. Gather those three crybabies still covering their heads on the ground and let's get out of here. I'm sorry about visiting without whistling first, Hank. It won't happen again."

"Make sure it doesn't." Hank was gruff as he stood in front of the barn doors. It was too dark to see inside, yet I was positive there was something else living in the ancient building. "If you come back, Tillie, come alone. The others aren't welcome."

"Not welcome by you?" I asked.

Hank scowled. "Not welcome by anyone. Now ... get out of here. I have things to do, and you're messing with my schedule."

"We're leaving," Thistle promised, her eyes troubled. "Be careful, Hank. The Feds are still out there."

"You might want to try following your own advice."

"Oh, we will. Don't worry about that."

ALIEN INSPIRATION

> Aliens would take one look at Aunt Tillie and run the other way. Even aliens aren't enough to stop her.
> **Clove on Aunt Tillie's power**

THIRTEEN

PROTECTING THE EARTH FROM THE SCUM OF THE PEWTER UNICORN STORE.

"He had something in the barn."

I waited until after we ditched Jace, Ryan and Morgan at Hollow Creek and we were on our way back to Hemlock Cove to state the obvious.

"What do you think he had in there?" Thistle asked from the back seat. Aunt Tillie called "shotgun" when we were still in the water, and the groaning about having to sit in the back was nonstop after that. Aunt Tillie was smug about the development as she set the controls so the heat blasted out of the vent at her feet, causing the rest of us to sweat.

"I have no idea what he has in there, but it's obviously something he doesn't want us to see," I replied, cracking my window to let some of the heat escape. Aunt Tillie was trying to sweat us out. "Something made that noise."

"Maybe it was an animal," Clove suggested. She didn't seem to be bothered by the heat. Instead of fanning herself, her eyes were closed and she looked as if she was about to sink into a nap. "Maybe he found Bigfoot."

"It's not Bigfoot." Thistle wrinkled her nose. "Good grief. I'm sick of hearing about you and Bigfoot. You need to let that go."

"You don't know." Clove's eyes snapped open. "It could be Bigfoot."

"I doubt very much that Bigfoot would allow itself to be hidden in a barn in the middle of nowhere," I pointed out pragmatically. "I guess it could've been a dog or something ... but I have no idea why Hank would be so dedicated to keeping a dog's identity secret."

"Maybe he stole the dog," Thistle suggested. "I think the Sandersons are looking for their dog. It went missing a few days ago."

"That little rat dog that looks like it has no fur?" I made a face. "Who would steal that dog?"

Thistle shrugged. "Maybe he thinks it's an alien."

That dog was funky-looking. "I think we should go back."

"Back to Hank's barn?" Clove turned shrill. "I don't want to go back to his barn."

"He doesn't have Bigfoot in there!" Thistle snapped. "How many times do I have to tell you that?"

"Until I believe it," Clove sneered. "I know what I know."

"And you know Bigfoot is in the barn?" I challenged.

"I think that's as likely as anything else." Clove refused to back down. "What else could it be?"

"An alien," Thistle replied without hesitation, refusing to look away when I snagged her gaze in the rearview mirror. "Oh, don't look at me that way. We were all thinking it. Hank's property is close to the crash site. If something escaped from the crash site ... ." She left it hanging, but following her rather obvious breadcrumbs was simple.

"I keep going back and forth on the alien thing," I admitted, pulling off the highway and heading toward town. "One second I think it's a ludicrous idea, and the next I believe it's possible aliens are running around the woods. I don't know what to make of it."

"Well, I think the idea of aliens is stupid even though I just said that it might be an alien," Thistle announced. "I'm leaning toward Bigfoot."

"You're only leaning toward Bigfoot because you know it will drive Clove crazy," I countered. "You don't believe Hank is keeping Bigfoot in his barn."

"I think Bigfoot is just as likely as aliens."

"Which means you think it's something else," I surmised, rolling my neck as I pulled into a parking spot in front of Hypnotic. "Maybe it really is the Sandersons' dog."

"Oh, I just had a terrible idea." Clove slowly unlatched her seatbelt and leaned forward. "What if he's not keeping a dog or an alien out there? What if he's keeping a person in his barn?"

I couldn't wrap my head around what she was saying. "What person? How did we jump to a person?" I flicked a gaze to Aunt Tillie, surprised she wasn't joining in the conversation. Her eyes were closed and she was breathing evenly, which meant she was asleep. The heat and the day's exertion were enough to force an unforeseen nap. I shouldn't have been surprised.

"How should I know what person it is?" Clove shot back. "Hank probably drove to another town and kidnapped a woman to act as his wife. That's who he's keeping in his barn."

Oh, good, we'd gotten to the "panic for no good reason" portion of the afternoon. It was only a matter of time. "So ... you think Hank drove to another town, kidnapped someone and is keeping her in his barn?"

Clove nodded solemnly.

"Does Hank even own a vehicle?"

"He's got that old beater truck," Thistle supplied. "I don't think it has a license plate or anything. I'm pretty sure he just uses it to drive around his property."

"He could've figured it out." Clove was adamant as she folded her arms over her chest. "I bet I'm right. I bet he kidnapped someone. We should probably tell Chief Terry so he can go out there and check."

That sounded like a terrible idea. "I think we would've heard if someone was missing. Stuff like that is big news up here. When Tina Clinton went quiet for two days because she had that boob lift everyone in town was looking for her within five hours. You can't keep anything secret around here, and that includes a disappearance."

AMANDA M. LEE

"I guess you're right." Clove didn't look happy as she broke off, chewing her bottom lip. The second her eyes sparked, I knew we were in trouble. "What if he didn't kidnap someone? What if he bought a mail-order bride and has her locked in his barn?"

Thistle snorted. "What?"

"It's not funny." Clove was serious as she played with her engagement ring. "I saw a thing on *Dateline* about human trafficking. The mail-order bride sites are basically legalized human trafficking. I bet that's what it is."

I stared at her for a long beat. "You watch way too much television. Has anyone ever told you that?"

"You'll be sorry when I tell Chief Terry what I suspect and I get all the accolades for pointing him toward a human-trafficking ring."

"Yeah, yeah." I opened the door and stepped out, making sure to leave the window open two inches so Aunt Tillie would have fresh air while she slept. I didn't bother to ease the door shut. I knew once Aunt Tillie started napping there was no waking her up without a bullhorn. "You're not telling Chief Terry anything. We're going out there ourselves to investigate after dark."

"Who is this 'we' you're talking about?" Clove instantly challenged. "I am not traipsing through the woods in the middle of the night to search a barn that might be hiding Bigfoot."

"You just said that you thought it was human trafficking," Thistle pointed out.

"It's either human trafficking or Bigfoot," Clove sniffed. "I'm fifty-fifty on it right now."

"Ugh. You're such a kvetch." Thistle lightly smacked the back of Clove's head before turning to face the police station. "What the heck?"

I followed her gaze, confusion washing through me when I realized that every parking spot in front of the building was taken ... and some by area news vans. "I don't understand," I said. "What's going on?"

"Look." Clove pointed toward the building's side patio. "What are all those people doing over there?"

I realized right away what was happening, although acknowledging what I saw wasn't easy. Agent Gibson, Chief Terry and Landon stood in a central location on the patio. They were surrounded by at least seven other media representatives — two with cameras — and Gibson was talking as the reporters asked questions and jotted down notes. "It's a news conference."

"News conference?" Thistle furrowed her brow. "Why would they be holding a news conference?"

"About the crash."

"Oh." Thistle's expression shifted to reflect sympathy as she cast me a sidelong look. "I'm sure it's not a big deal."

Always the last to catch on, Clove voiced her confusion before thinking it through. "You're with the press," she pointed out. "Why weren't you invited?"

I pressed the tip of my tongue against the back of my teeth and shrugged. My emotions were completely out of control at this point, and I couldn't decide if I wanted to scream or cry. "I guess there's only one way to find out."

I picked an unhurried pace to cross the street even though I wanted to race to Gibson and smack him across the face. I knew that wouldn't earn me any points, so I purposely stepped lightly. By the time we erased the distance, the conference was breaking up and the other reporters were scattering.

Landon's was the first gaze I met. He looked ridiculously upset. "Where have you been?"

I ignored the question. "What was that?"

Gibson looked me up and down. "Who are you again?"

I gritted my teeth to keep from screaming. "Bay Winchester."

"She owns The Whistler," Landon volunteered. "The town paper."

"The town *weekly* paper." Gibson's eyes flashed with amusement as he shook his head. "I've seen that paper. It's an advertorial."

"It is not," I protested, my temper coming out to play. "Sure, we have a lot of advertisements. We also fill our news hole every week. It's a real paper."

"If you say so." Gibson flicked his eyes to Chief Terry. "I was thinking we could hit the diner for a late lunch and to discuss our next step. How does that sound?"

Chief Terry looked caught. "Well ... ."

"We're not done here," I interjected, slowly drawing Gibson's attention back to me. "I want to know why you had a conference without alerting me that it was taking place."

"It's not my job to alert you to anything, young lady." Gibson turned stern. "News releases were sent out alerting area media representatives that we would be holding a conference. It's not my fault you missed the notification."

"But ... ." I shook my head. "No. I get emails on my phone. I know whenever anything is emailed to The Whistler."

"I don't believe that particular newspaper was included on the notification list, although I could be wrong. My secretary sent out the notifications. I didn't do it personally." Gibson was imperious as he looked down on me. "I believe only television and daily newspapers were notified."

"What?"

"That's not fair," Landon interjected quickly. "She's just as diligent about her job as those other outlets. If you purposely left her out of the notifications, that's ... it's not fair."

"Life isn't fair, Agent Michaels." Gibson shot him a withering look. "Why do you care anyway?"

Landon's jaw muscle twitched as his eyes narrowed. "Because she's my girlfriend. We've already had this discussion."

"Oh, right. I believe that discussion started with me pointing out that an FBI agent should never date a member of the media because it's a conflict of interest. You stopped participating in the conversation not long after that."

"That doesn't mean I think you're right." Landon's temper was close to the surface. He was about to get himself in a lot of trouble. "If you purposely left her out ... ."

"I didn't purposely leave anyone out," Gibson snapped. "I didn't make the decision on who to notify. If you have a problem with that, take it up with the home office."

"I just might do that."

"Go ahead." Gibson made a dismissive face before turning to Chief Terry. "Where did we land on lunch?"

Chief Terry boasted Landon's same foul mood. "I don't have much of an appetite."

"Oh, well, your loss." Gibson shrugged before stepping around me. "I'm going to lunch. I'll see you gentlemen in an hour. I expect you'll have ideas on the next stage of operation at that time." He briefly glanced at me. "Don't waste your time on the media, please. That part of our day is over."

Landon barely managed to contain himself until Gibson was out of earshot. The second the prickly man disappeared inside the diner, he exploded. "Where have you been?"

I inadvertently stepped back in the face of his vehemence. "Excuse me?"

"I'm sorry." Landon immediately held his hands up in apology. "I didn't mean to yell. I've been trying to reach you for two hours. You didn't answer any of my texts. I knew he was trying to keep you out of it the second he mentioned it."

"You texted?" That was news to me. I dug into my pocket for my phone. It showed a litany of missed texts — almost all of them from Landon (although a few were from Chief Terry) — and each one urged that I get back to town right away. "Oh. You did text. My phone was on silent this afternoon. I didn't realize."

"We tried to get in touch with you, sweetheart." Chief Terry looked pained. "I even called the inn in the hopes that your mother would be able to track you down. She said Tillie was missing, too, and assumed you were all together."

"Aunt Tillie is sleeping in the car." I gestured vaguely. "She was tired after our adventure."

"Plus, she cranked up the heat so the car was a sauna," Thistle added. "It was only a matter of time until she took a nap."

"You can't leave her in the car," Landon groused. "I know it's only spring, but she could die in there."

"We cracked the windows."

"Good thinking." Landon's expression was plaintive as he focused on me. "I'm sorry. I tried to reach you. I didn't know what else to do."

As angry as I was, it wasn't directed at him. "It's not your fault. You did your best. I was busy with other stuff, otherwise I'm sure I would've seen the texts."

"What other stuff?" Chief Terry asked. "Do we even want to know what you were up to?"

"Given Agent Gibson's dislike of me, I don't think it's wise to tell you what we were doing," I answered honestly. "It's not that I think you'll blab as much as I don't want you put in a position where you'll get in trouble if you don't blab."

"I'm beyond caring about that right now," Landon countered. "I'm sorry you were cut out of this. I'm upset on your behalf."

That was clearly true. Oddly enough, it made me feel better. "I'm okay. I'm guessing he didn't say anything of note in the conference anyway."

Landon and Chief Terry exchanged a look. It was furtive ... and weighted.

"Well ... ." Landon shifted from one foot to the other as he shifted his eyes to me.

"There were a few things of note in the conference," Chief Terry said finally. "All the points were handed out in a printed release. And we're not allowed to comment on any of it."

Oh, well, that just figured. "You can't tell me what was said at the conference?"

"Almost nothing was said, Bay," Landon replied. "You need to get your hands on the information sheet ... and we can't give it to you. You'll have to convince Gibson to hand it over, but I don't think he'll do it simply because you ask nicely. He seems to have attitude about me ... and he's carried it over to you. I'm sorry for that."

He looked so earnest I couldn't hold out in the face of his misery. "Don't worry about it." I squeezed his hand. "Have you considered that he has attitude about you because of me?"

"He seemed to have attitude with me from the start. That was long before you were even mentioned."

"That doesn't mean he didn't know about me," I pressed. "It's not as if our relationship is on the down low."

"No, but I don't think it matters." Landon dragged a restless hand through his hair. "He won't willingly give you that news release. You might have to go through the home office to get it."

"Don't worry about that." I waved off his concern. "That release is the least of my worries. Just for the record, I might be sneaking out of the guesthouse again tonight. In an effort to keep the lying to a minimum, I'm warning you now."

"I don't want you running around the woods alone at night," Landon complained.

"I won't be alone."

"Oh, I don't like it when you say things like that," Clove whined. "I don't want to go with you. I object."

"We're not in court, moron," Thistle snapped. "Good grief. You're such a whiner." She exhaled heavily as she flicked her eyes back to my car. The passenger door was open and Aunt Tillie was standing next to it, a dazed look on her face. "Good morning, sunshine," Thistle chirped. "We're so glad you could join us."

Aunt Tillie's expression was blank. "What did I miss?"

ALIEN INSPIRATION

> Why would I want to go to space? I guarantee there's no bacon in space. Sure, they might have something else, but I'm not taking that risk.
>
> **Landon on why he isn't keen on space travel**

FOURTEEN

PART WOMAN. PART WITCH. ALL MAYHEM. THE FUTURE OF MAGIC.

*L*andon insisted on walking me back to the newspaper. It was obvious he wanted us to have some time alone, but my mind was so busy I could barely focus on him.

"I'm sorry."

I pulled up short when I inserted my key in the door and turned to face him. "What are you sorry about?"

Landon was plaintive. "I tried to call you. I was livid when I realized Gibson planned to hold a news conference without you. I argued with him, but he wouldn't budge."

That's when I realized Landon was taking this whole thing to heart more so than me, which wasn't exactly healthy. "It's okay." I patted his arm and then directed him inside. "You didn't do this. I'm not upset."

Landon's expression was dubious. "You're not upset? Why don't I believe that?"

"I don't know." I shut the door and started down the hallway, doing an about-face when I realized I was heading in the wrong direction. "My office is this way now."

I pointed my finger, which Landon proceeded to catch as he stared hard into my eyes. "How can you not be upset? He was mean to you."

I shrugged. "I spent the day with Aunt Tillie. Mean is a state of mind."

Landon barked out a laugh. "I love you ... ridiculously." He pulled me in for a hug and blew out a sigh as he rested his cheek on my forehead. "I can't take much more of this."

I decided to approach it from a rational direction. "Oh, yeah?" I pulled back so I could study his face. "What are you going to do to change the situation?"

"I thought I might quit my job and live on love."

Now it was my turn to snort. "That's cute."

"I'm serious." Landon's face didn't crack. "I'll quit the FBI and become your love slave. You own a business now. You can be the primary breadwinner."

"I hate to point out the obvious, but I'm the lone reporter in this town, and I wasn't invited to an important news conference. I'm not sure how long I can keep us afloat."

"Ugh." Landon went back to hugging me, swaying back and forth as he growled. "I hate that guy. I mean ... I really hate him. I hate him so much I want to pull an Aunt Tillie, drive him to the woods, and use a whistle when I hunt him."

"That's kind of weird."

"Yeah, well ... whatever." Landon gave me a soft kiss before heaving a sigh and taking a step back. "What were you doing today that you missed all my texts? Your phone should have been pinging like crazy."

Ah. We were delving into dangerous territory here. "I was out with a few people."

Landon cocked an eyebrow. "Thistle, Clove and Aunt Tillie. I know. I saw you."

"A few other people besides that," I hedged. I didn't want to lie — having a relationship built on trust wasn't easy if you were constantly lying — but telling the truth could get me in trouble. I hated getting in trouble.

Landon recognized right away that I was averting my eyes and grew suspicious. "Who were you with?"

"Well ... ."

"Bay, I'm not going to bust you for this," Landon said. "I feel guilty because you were cut out of the news conference. I'll let you get away with murder no matter what."

I brightened considerably. "Good point." I beamed at him. "We were searching for information on what happened in Potter's Field this morning — people report stuff like that on various blogs — and we stumbled across a group of people who we thought might have information."

That was appropriately vague, right? I can never tell.

Landon narrowed his eyes. "I'll need more information than that. Who is this group of people?"

"If I tell you, I'm fairly certain all that guilt you're feeling will dry up and I won't get my massage later."

"What massage?"

"The one I'm going to force you to give me so I'll feel better about being cut out of the conference."

"Uh-huh." Landon's expression was hard to read. Over the eighteen months we'd spent together I'd come to recognize exactly what he was feeling by the way he held his face, but he was a mystery today. "Bay, who were you with?"

"Fine." I dragged a hand through my hair. "There are these three guys who run a blog called 'Aliens Among Us' and they happened to be staying at the Dragonfly. We headed out there to see what they knew — and have lunch with our fathers, which didn't go all that well — and then we all took a walk in the woods together."

Landon was shocked. "Wait a second ... !"

"You held a news conference without me," I reminded him, pressing my advantage.

"Knock that off." Landon wrapped his hands around my wrists as he processed the information. "Why didn't lunch with your father go well?"

The question caught me off guard. "Oh, well ... they think we're nutty to be looking at the alien stuff, too. It didn't help that Aunt Tillie followed us, invited herself for French Dip sandwiches, and then dripped au jus sauce down her shirt. Dad doesn't find her half as endearing as I do."

Landon snorted. "You had a French Dip for lunch? That sounds good. I haven't eaten since breakfast."

"I'm sorry. I stopped carrying bacon around in my pockets to entice you because it was attracting area dogs. I don't have anything to offer by way of a snack."

"Ha, ha." Landon slowly released my wrists. "Tell me about these guys. I'm not keen on you going into the woods with strangers."

"I wouldn't worry about it. They're about nineteen and complete morons."

"I figured that out when you told me the name of the blog."

"Hey, you don't know aliens aren't out there," I argued, remembering the look on Hank's face when whatever was in his barn decided to make a noise. "There could be aliens out there."

"I thought you were determined it was a drone," Landon challenged.

Something occurred to me. "Is it a drone? Can you confirm that?"

"I can't confirm anything, and you know it. I haven't even seen the wreckage myself. Gibson has me filling out paperwork for things I haven't seen and answering phones. I'm a glorified secretary."

"Oh, poor baby." I lightly patted his behind before giving it a squeeze. "You can be my secretary and I'll sexually harass you."

"That's not funny." Landon slid out of my grip. "Although ... I'm willing to play that game later if you bring me a bouquet of bacon to celebrate Secretary's Day."

"Good to know."

"As for the rest, I don't know what to tell you." Landon's eyes darkened. "I am frustrated to the point I want to go to bed the rest of the week and forget about this. I don't like not being in charge."

He said the words as if it were some big revelation. It took everything I had to hold back a laugh. "No. I never would've guessed that."

"I know you're being sarcastic, but it's true. I want to be in charge. I'm used to being in charge. I don't do well when I'm not in charge."

"You sound like Aunt Tillie."

"You mean that as an insult, but I don't think she's wrong on this front," he countered. "Not being in charge is the worst."

He sounded like a petulant child, but for some reason it warmed my heart. "You can boss me around later if you want. We can definitely play the secretary game."

"I would rather have things back to normal. You know ... like when we work together. This case blows."

"It definitely blows," I agreed. "We both have to do what we have to do, though. I'm sure this will be over within a day or so. They're already wrapping up the search at the crash site."

Landon stilled, his eyes clouding. "How do you know that?"

Crap. "How do you think? I mean ... I pretty much told you when I explained about how we were hanging with the bloggers."

"You were out there." Landon's answer was simple, although his tone was shrill. "How do you keep getting out there without anyone seeing you? It was one thing to do it at night. We didn't get that close and no one was looking that far into the woods. But now you're doing it in the day. How are you doing it without being caught?"

"Oh, I can't tell you that." I tapped my finger on the end of his nose. "That's a secret of the trade. I can't tell 'The Man' my secrets in case you hold it against me in court."

Landon scowled. "You know I'd never do that."

"It was a joke. I also recognize that what you don't know can't hurt you. It's better if I don't tell you how I'm getting out there."

"Fine." Landon didn't look happy, but he dropped it. "I know you said you were going on an adventure after dark tonight, but is there a chance we can share dinner before that?"

"Absolutely."

"Good." He dropped an affectionate kiss on my forehead. "I'll be in touch."

ONCE LANDON LEFT — which he was reluctant to do — I focused on my inbox. Sure enough, the FBI had sent a news release at 9:36 a.m. Why I didn't see it on my phone, I couldn't say. It was too late to dwell on that, so I simply pushed it out of my mind. I would find the information another way. I had no doubt about that.

In addition to the news conference notification, I found I had at least fifteen people messaging to say they had photographs of the crash. Some wanted me to buy the photos — one guy was even asking six figures — but some were offering their photos for free. They simply wanted a photo credit. I focused on those.

"Huh." Most of the photos were taken with cell phones, so the quality wasn't great. It didn't help that the incident happened late in the day, so there was some lens flare on a few of the images. The photos taken once darkness fell showed flames in a field and nothing else. There was one set, though, that was better quality than the rest. These were taken with a telephoto lens and I could actually make out some metal framework in a few of the shots.

"That's interesting," I murmured to myself as I tapped my lip. "That definitely doesn't look like a plane."

"What doesn't look like a plane?" Viola, the newspaper office's resident ghost, popped into existence at my left elbow, causing me to nearly jolt out of my skin. "What are you looking at?"

I tamped down my irritation and stretched as I bartered for time to calm myself. "Hello, Viola."

"Hello." Viola was bright-eyed and happy as she stared at my computer. "Seriously, what are you looking at?"

I tried to remind myself that Viola was a vast improvement over the last ghost who haunted the newspaper offices. Sure, she was annoying and sometimes said inane things, but she wasn't terrible. She wasn't judgmental and blatantly racist or anything. That was a big step up from the former ghost, Edith, who never met a terrible opinion she didn't want to hold.

"These are photographs from the incident at Potter's Field," I explained after a beat. "Have you heard about that?"

Viola nodded, solemn. "They say it's aliens."

I was taken aback. "Who says it's aliens? Have you been hanging around Aunt Tillie?"

"Only when I'm in the mood to see if I can get her blood pressure to spike," Viola replied. "Everyone in town is talking about it. They say that aliens landed in the field and the government is hiding it."

This was news to me. I thought the only ones considering such a ridiculous idea shared Winchester DNA. "What are they saying?"

"A lot of different things. Doris Andrews swears up and down she saw creatures with glowing eyes hiding in her bushes. She called Terry, but he told her she was imagining things even though she described the masks the aliens wore to perfection."

That didn't make sense. "What masks?"

"You know. Eye masks." Viola demonstrated with her ethereal hands. "Aliens can wear masks. There's no rule."

I rolled the idea through my head. "Are you sure she wasn't looking at raccoons?"

"Why would it be raccoons?"

"Because their eyes seem to glow in the dark at times."

"Hmm." Viola turned thoughtful. "I didn't really consider that. She did say the glowing eyes were close to her trash bins. I guess that makes sense."

"Yeah." I rolled my neck as I turned back to the photos. "Does that look like a plane to you?"

Viola followed my gaze. "Not any plane I've ever seen."

"I know. It's something else."

"Flying saucer?"

"I'm leaning toward drone."

"Drones are tiny. You can control them with joysticks and stuff. I've seen them at Target ... you know, back when I was alive."

"There are different types of drones." I scratched my temple and shifted my eyes to the window when I caught a hint of movement out of the corner of my eye. "What the heck was that?"

"What?" Viola was more interested in the photograph on my laptop than the great outdoors. She didn't bother looking up. "I don't see anything out of the ordinary in this photo."

AMANDA M. LEE

"No, I wasn't talking about that." I slowly got to my feet and moved to the window, pressing my forehead against the glass and gazing out. A furtive shadow disappeared around the far corner of the building before I could make out a figure. "Huh. I'll be right back."

I left Viola with my computer and headed toward the back door. When I had taken over the newspaper, Landon made sure to change all the locks because he wanted to make sure no one could get inside while I worked. He was especially concerned about the rear door, which tended to stick and give the illusion of being locked when it wasn't. That was the door I opened now. The two people I saw standing on the other side of the threshold were not ones I expected.

"Mrs. Little?"

Mrs. Little flashed a bright smile, although her eyes looked unfocused. I couldn't decide if she really was acting differently or I was simply projecting my inner worry on her. It was a fifty-fifty proposition. "Hello, Bay. It's a lovely day, isn't it?"

I'd never known Mrs. Little to be fixated on the weather so much. Sure, she worried when we had an upcoming festival, but she never gave it much thought otherwise. She'd mentioned it several times the past few days, and it was odd.

"Yeah, it's great." I licked my lips and studied the woman with Mrs. Little. Oddly enough, it was the same woman Viola was talking about only moments before. "Hi, Doris. I'm surprised to see you hanging about today. I heard you had an otherworldly visit to your garbage cans this week."

Doris merely shrugged. "How did you hear that?"

"I can't exactly remember," I lied. "Someone told me. I wish I could remember who."

"Yes, well, I was mistaken." Doris was more succinct than normal, her eyes roaming my face but never settling. "I thought I saw something outside, but it turned out to be nothing."

"I thought maybe it was raccoons."

"Yes, raccoons." Doris bobbed her head. "I'm sure it was raccoons. May we come inside?"

The harsh transition was enough to jar me. "You want to come inside the newspaper office?"

"Why else would we be here?"

"I don't know." I flicked my eyes to Mrs. Little. "Are you here for a specific reason? I mean ... do you need something? Are you feeling all right?"

"We're here to see you," Mrs. Little said, her stiff smile remaining in place. "We've been visiting various business owners. You're next on our list."

"But ... why?"

"We're simply enjoying the spring day."

Mrs. Little's response was almost robotic. It set my teeth on edge. "Well ... that's interesting and a little weird. I'm busy."

Mrs. Little's eyes gleamed. "Busy doing what?"

"Working."

"On what?"

Was she kidding me? "On newspaper stuff." My gaze bounced between both empty faces, and I couldn't help feeling uncomfortable. "Are you sure you're feeling okay?"

"I'm great." Mrs. Little squared her shoulders. "Why wouldn't I be great? It's spring and it's a fine day."

"It's a pip of a day," Doris agreed. "We would really like to come inside and look around, maybe sit down with you and share some ... good conversation."

If I thought this particular meeting of the minds was odd before, that was nothing compared to the discomfort rolling through me now. "Well ... I'd love to sit down with you, but I have other things to deal with. They really can't wait. How about we set up an appointment to talk about things?"

"That sounds lovely," Doris enthused. "Are you free in twenty minutes?"

"No. I was thinking more like next week."

Doris immediately started shaking her head. "That's not going to work for me."

"It's the best I can do." I remained firm. "I'm sorry if that doesn't work for you, but I have a schedule. I can't break from it."

"That doesn't work for me," Doris repeated, turning to face Mrs. Little without making eye contact. "That doesn't work for us, right?"

"No." Mrs. Little clutched her hands together and shook her head. "That doesn't work or us. We need to spend time with you today."

The more they talked, the antsier I felt. "I'm sorry you feel that way, but ... I'm out of time. I'll text you when I can squeeze you in. How does that sound?"

"It's not going to work for us," Mrs. Little repeated. "Not at all."

She sounded like a skipping record. "Okay, well, we'll figure something out. You should probably continue enjoying your day. I'll text you later." I hurriedly shut the door and locked it, not caring in the least that I probably came off as rude. Mrs. Little was used to me being rude.

When I turned, I found Viola hovering behind me.

"Well, that was weird," she said. "What's up with Margaret?"

I shrugged. "I have no idea. That was straight out of an alien movie."

"I told you it was aliens."

"I'm not sure it is, but something weird is going on here. We need to find out what."

ALIEN INSPIRATION

> I'm the Captain Kirk of FBI agents. Whenever someone says it can't be done, I prove them wrong. I also over-enunciate when I'm trying to make a point. It's a trade-off.
>
> **Landon on living a *Star Trek* life**

FIFTEEN

MAY THE HOCUS POCUS BE WITH YOU.

I was nervous when it came time to leave The Whistler.

For some reason — and I knew it was ridiculous — I couldn't shake the odd way Mrs. Little had been acting. Something was seriously off. And, while accepting that aliens might be to blame made me look like an idiot, that also seemed to plug a few plot holes in the ongoing narrative.

I walked the building, checking every window for hints of movement, and then sat at the empty front desk and called Landon. He answered on the third ring.

"If you've decided to think better of it and want to be angry about earlier, I won't allow it," he said by way of greeting. "I can't take another argument."

He sounded wearier than I felt. "I don't want to argue."

"Good. What's up?"

"Where are you?" I tried to sound casual, but my heart skipped a beat when I saw a shadow move past one of the windows. Most likely it belonged to a bush ... or the budding leaves ... or maybe even a flag. I couldn't get the idea of Mrs. Little and Doris as pod people attacking me.

"I'm at the station." Landon sounded bored with the conversation. "Where are you?"

"The Whistler."

"Still? I thought you'd have finished up hours ago. Are you heading home? I can meet you for dinner at the inn if you want."

"They're having steak tonight," I said automatically.

"I like steak."

"It's not your favorite. I thought maybe we could hit the diner. We'll be able to get in and out without being caught up in family drama." And spend some time alone, I added silently.

Landon was silent for a long time. I could practically hear his mind working through the call. "We can eat at the diner. That sounds good."

"Great."

"I can be there in twenty minutes."

"Okay."

Landon waited for me to say more. When I didn't, he filled the silence. "Sweetie, is there something going on you want to tell me about?"

I chewed my bottom lip, undecided. Was there? Should I tell him about this? He would laugh at my reaction. There was no getting around that. I couldn't shake the worry, and regret was impossible to live with. If I didn't put my plan into action, there was a chance I would always be surrounded by regret.

"I need you to do something for me," I said finally.

"Is it something dirty?"

"No, but I'll add something dirty to the mix if you do what I ask without questioning me," I offered, hopeful.

"What do you want me to do?" Landon sounded intrigued. That wouldn't stop him from making fun of me if the chance arose.

"I'm going to ask you to do something that you'll think is strange," I started, choosing my words carefully. "I'm going to ask you to do it anyway and I don't want any lip."

"Ooh, I'm all tingly with anticipation."

He was clearly enjoying himself. That didn't stop me from laying it all out for him.

"I had a scary situation here earlier," I explained. "You won't think it's scary — so don't even bother asking about it — but I think it's scary. Now I'm worried Mrs. Little is hanging around outside the newspaper office. I need you to park by the back door.

"I'll keep watch for when you arrive, which will allow me to slip outside and run to your vehicle," I continued. "You stay inside the Explorer and I'll hop in the passenger side, and then I want you to take off as fast as you can."

It was so quiet on the other end of the call I thought I'd lost him.

"Landon?"

"I'm here." All traces of mirth were gone. "Do you want to tell me what this is about?"

"Over dinner."

"Maybe I don't want to wait."

I bit back a sigh. He was such a pain in the keister when he wanted to be. "Landon, I know I sound like a loon. I freely admit that I might be losing my mind. That doesn't change the fact that I need you to do this."

"And you're going to tell me why you need me to do this over dinner, right?"

I wasn't keen on that, but saw no other option. "Yes."

"Fine. Get ready." I could tell Landon was resigned as I heard him shuffling things around his desk on the other end of the call. "I'll be there in four minutes. If I see someone chasing you, prepare yourself. I will break the terms of our agreement and jump out to save you."

Hopefully, that wouldn't be necessary. "It's probably nothing." I offered him a hollow laugh that sounded unnecessarily harsh. "Sometimes I work myself up and I can't explain it."

"I'm well aware of that. I'm on my way."

"I'll be ready."

I double checked the front door before moving to the back. I hoped Mrs. Little would assume I was leaving through the front. I had every intention of abandoning my vehicle in favor of Landon's if it meant escape.

I peered through the small window at the side of the door and waited. Everything appeared calm on the other side of the door, but that didn't stop my heart from pounding. The second I saw Landon's truck I threw open the door and stepped outside.

I wasn't exactly a natural athlete — I blamed my mother ... and aunts ... and especially Aunt Tillie — but I managed to keep my hands steady as I locked the door. I didn't trip as I descended the stairs, my eyes busy as they bounced around looking for attackers.

It took me two tries to open the passenger door of Landon's Explorer, but once inside I heaved out a sigh as I locked the door and stared into the foliage near the woods. I'd made it. That was good. My plan worked.

Landon didn't immediately drive away. When I slid my eyes to him, I found his hands gripping the steering wheel tightly and his expression grim. "What was that, Bay? Who is following you?"

I was expecting the question. That didn't mean I was ready to answer. "Just ... go. I'll tell you once I've settled."

"Tell me now. If someone has threatened you ... ." He trailed off and I recognized the uncertainty weighing him down. "Did Gibson say something to you? I warned him to stay away from you."

Hmm. That was interesting. It seemed Landon was worked up regarding his own matters. "It has nothing to do with Agent Gibson."

"Are you sure?"

"Yes. You're going to think I'm an idiot when I tell you what happened."

"I doubt that." Landon quickly squeezed my hand before putting the vehicle in gear. "You're going to tell me everything over dinner. I know we have a deal stating otherwise because of the situation, but I'm changing that deal. I want to go back to the way things were."

"What about Agent Gibson?"

"Screw him."

I widened my eyes. That did not sound like the Landon I knew. "Really?"

"Really." He checked the rearview mirror. "We have a lot to talk about."

Apparently, we did.

LANDON CHOSE A BOOTH in the corner for privacy for our big discussion. He waited until after we received our iced teas and had placed our orders to ask the obvious question.

"What happened to you today?"

I met his serious gaze and shrugged. "You're going to laugh."

"No, I'm not. I saw the look on your face when you escaped from the building. You were genuinely afraid."

That was a mild exaggeration. "I wasn't afraid. I was careful."

"It seemed like more than that to me."

It would, of course. He was in tune with my emotions, even more so lately since I started controlling the dead and seemingly talking to myself during random parts of the day. He didn't bring that up now, but I realized that's what he was really worried about.

"I think there's something weird going on with Mrs. Little," I explained after a beat. "I mean ... like really weird."

To give himself time, Landon sipped his iced tea and studied me. "What do you think is wrong with Mrs. Little?" he asked finally.

"I don't know. It's possible she's simply messing with me. Given how Aunt Tillie has treated her over the years — and, yes, I was a willing participant for most of it — I would have it coming if she ever decided to pay me back."

"Fair enough." Landon steepled his hands and waited. "Tell me."

There was no way out of it. I was succinct and to the point. When I was done, instead of laughing Landon cocked his head to the side.

"Are you saying that she's acting weird enough that you're actually considering Aunt Tillie's *Invasion of the Body Snatchers* scenario?"

Well, when he put it like that ... . "You don't need to sound so dismissive," I said. "It's simply one hypothesis."

"And what are the others?"

"That she's had a stroke and somehow it's changed her personality for the better," I answered without hesitation. "Oh, and there's the possibility that she's simply playing an elaborate hoax to get back at Aunt Tillie. Like I said, we have it coming."

"And why aren't you leaning toward that possibility?"

"Because it takes dedication and imagination. Mrs. Little has dedication, but she's lacking in imagination. And she's not smart enough to come up with an idea like this."

Landon stroked his chin as he studied me. "I don't want to encourage you — that actually sounds very dangerous right now — but you have a point. I can see Aunt Tillie coming up with this scenario to drive Mrs. Little crazy. I cannot see Mrs. Little being fun enough to come up with something like this to mess with you guys."

"It would almost be a relief if she could," I admitted. "But you're right, she's not fun enough. That's why she's always such an easy mark for Aunt Tillie."

"I can see that." Landon leaned back in the booth, his eyes solemn. "Do you really think it's aliens?"

I hated being put on the spot. "I really think Agent Gibson is hiding something," I answered carefully. "When you put all the pieces together, it makes a compelling picture ... and that picture just might happen to have aliens in it."

Landon's expression didn't change. "Put all the pieces together for me."

I didn't immediately react. "I thought we agreed to keep our investigations separate on this one."

"I already told you, I'm over that." He was firm. "I don't want to be separated from you any longer. We're going to figure this out together."

"But ... Agent Gibson won't like it if you share information."

"I don't have any information to share. He's kept everything from me. He wants me close to act as a shield with the locals because I'm a familiar face. Other than that, I don't know what's going on."

"Nothing?"

"Nothing."

I furrowed my brow. "That can't be right," I said finally, running the scenario through my head. "You've been working with him for days. You must know something."

"Bay, all he's told Chief Terry and me is that there was an incident,"

Landon supplied. "He said that it was a military operation and only those with top security clearance could see the reports. That does not include me."

My heart went out to him. "I'm sorry he's such a jerk."

Landon's lips curved. "I'm sorry he's such a jerk, too, but I'm over it. I'm sick of being left in the dark."

"That's why you didn't put up a bigger objection when I snuck out of the guesthouse," I mused. "You were hoping I would stumble across something that could help you fill in the gaps."

"Basically," Landon conceded. "Gibson isn't sharing ... and I'm done being kept out of the loop."

"So, what are you suggesting?"

"That we work together."

"How?"

"I haven't figured that out yet," Landon conceded. "I have a few ideas if you're willing to listen."

I was officially intrigued. "Okay, what have you got?"

"For starters, I thought we could get Aunt Tillie to cast a spell – or maybe even concoct a potion – that we can use to knock Gibson out." Landon was serious as he rubbed his hands together. "Then we'll break into his room at whatever bed and breakfast he's staying and go through all of his files."

It was a ridiculously simple plan. It was also immediate grounds for him to be fired ... and probably locked up for the rest of his life. "That would make you an accessory to drugging a federal agent. Also, I'm pretty sure going through his stuff is against the law."

"Oh, look who is suddenly a fan of following the letter of the law," Landon muttered, annoyance on full display.

"Hey, I didn't say I wanted to follow the law. That's a horrible thing to say."

Landon's lips quirked. "Fine. What's your plan?"

"I have several ideas," I admitted, grabbing a roll from the basket at the center of the table and ripping the top off and shoving it in my mouth. When I swallowed, I had my emotions under more control.

"The thing is, I'm familiar with a way to get back to the scene that Gibson doesn't know about."

"I already figured that out," Landon admitted. "I haven't mentioned anything to Gibson because I don't want you arrested — and I actually like it when you make him look like an idiot — but I've known that since the second day."

"Well, we were out there again today," I offered. "We ran into Hank William Jenkins."

Landon was blasé. "Is that a real name?"

"His father was a big fan of a certain country music star."

"Only in Hemlock Cove."

"I think that probably could've happened anywhere," I countered. "The thing is, Hank is something of a loon. He lives out in the woods by himself. He has no running water. He's one of those preppers who has a bunker and is readying himself for the end of the world."

"Zombies?"

"Apparently this time it's aliens."

Landon snickered, seemingly enjoying himself. "I never thought this would become an actual conversation between us. Sure, we had fun with the idea of an alien invasion, but you're treating it as a real thing."

"I still think it's far more likely that a drone crashed." I felt the need to cover my bases. "There's other stuff going on. I can't ignore it."

"Fine." Landon held up his hands in capitulation. "Tell me what happened at Hank William Jenkins' house this afternoon. Did he tell you about how country boys survive?"

"No. He almost shot us because he doesn't like trespassers. Then we found out he has some weird relationship with Aunt Tillie and he backed off. None of us knew they hung out."

Landon leaned forward. "Wait ... what?"

"It's true. They're buddies."

"Like ... sex buddies?"

I scorched him with a dark look. "Not sex buddies! Don't be gross."

"How was I supposed to know?"

"You don't always have to jump to the gross conclusion."

"Fair enough." Landon's smile was mischievous. "So Aunt Tillie and the town loner have a unique relationship. Continue."

"It's more than that. He was acting weird — even weirder than normal, according to Aunt Tillie — and we heard a noise in his barn. He wouldn't allow us to see what was in there, but he's hiding something."

"An alien?"

I shrugged. "Something. We're going back tonight to find out what."

Landon feigned patience. "Have you ever considered that it might be a horse ... or a cow ... or a goat?"

"He lives, like, a quarter of a mile from the crash scene. He's in the middle of the woods."

Landon licked his lips. I could practically see his mind working. "I'm not saying that I believe it's aliens," he said finally.

"But you believe it's worth taking a look," I finished, amused. "You want to see what Hank has in his barn as much as we do."

"I'm interested. Let's leave it at that."

"I'm taking Clove, Thistle and Aunt Tillie with me. This is a Winchester thing, and I'm inviting you along out of the goodness of my heart. If you turn all FBI agent and threaten to start arresting everyone, you won't be invited back a second time."

Instead of being offended, Landon let loose a low chuckle. "Seems like a fair deal."

I waited, but he didn't add to the statement. "That's it? You're not going to push things further?"

"No. I want us to be a team again."

Honestly, I wanted it, too. I missed working together for the common good. "Okay. We'll eat dinner, maybe have some ice cream, and wait until it's dark to head to Hank's house."

Landon's smile was crooked when he stretched his legs under the table. "Have you given any thought to what you'll do if you actually find an alien?"

"Probably run and scream."

"Well, at least you have a plan."

"That's the most important thing," I agreed. "We'll figure out the rest as we go along."

"Bay?"

"Hmm."

"It's a pleasure to be on your team again."

I couldn't resist his charming grin. "Right back at you."

ALIEN INSPIRATION

" You know that scene in *Alien* where the little monster punches out of that guy's chest and tries to kill them all? That's how I feel when Aunt Tillie says she has an idea.

Thistle trying to talk everyone out of helping Aunt Tillie with her most recent plan

SIXTEEN

BOLDLY GO WHERE NO WITCH HAS GONE BEFORE.

Landon followed my instructions after dinner and parked at Hollow Creek. We were the first to arrive, and he was thoughtful as we exited his Explorer.

"I didn't even think about entering from this direction," he mused, his expression serious as he stared at the water. "Gibson said he had all the angles covered to keep people away from the scene. He mentioned that one side was cut off by water. I didn't realize which body of water he was referring to until now."

"You're not as familiar with the area," I offered helpfully. "It's not your fault."

"Chief Terry should have realized. He knows the area."

"Maybe he didn't think about it."

"Or maybe he chose to keep his mouth shut because he wanted to see what you would uncover," Landon countered. "I'm seriously impressed, Bay. Approaching from this direction was smart. You're either a genius or a criminal mastermind."

"I prefer genius."

"Fair enough."

AMANDA M. LEE

Thistle arrived with Aunt Tillie a few minutes later. I texted before leaving the diner to make sure that someone was available to pick up our crotchety great-aunt. Clove was coming from the opposite direction, so it only made sense to saddle Thistle with the deed.

"I'm not doing that, you old crank!" Thistle slammed the door as she exited her car and fixed me with a dark look. "She's going back with you when we're finished tonight. I'm not kidding."

Landon's smile was lazy as he hooked his fingers in his belt loops and rocked back on his heels. "And it's lovely to see you this evening, too, Thistle."

Thistle ignored his sarcasm and remained focused on me. "She's being a real pill. She's your responsibility now."

Aunt Tillie was slower getting out of the car. When she exited I realized she was wearing her combat helmet and boots. She was also holding a shotgun.

"You can't take that with you." I hurriedly scampered around the car, every intention of wrestling the gun out of her hands.

Anticipating my reaction, Aunt Tillie took an exaggerated step back and glared. "Don't even think about it. I have a constitutional right to bear arms."

"Not when we're walking through the woods in the dark," I argued. "You could trip and shoot someone ... or yourself."

"We're more worried about you shooting someone else," Thistle interjected, her eyes landing on Landon. "What's he doing here?"

"It's always a pleasure to spend time with you, too, Thistle," Landon drawled. "The warmth with which you regard me is so profound it causes my soul to want to sing."

I cocked an eyebrow. "That was a little over the top."

"I heard it as I was saying it," Landon acknowledged. "It was already too late to take it back."

As a Winchester, I understood that Foot In Mouth Disease was real, so I let it go. "Aunt Tillie, you can't take that gun."

Aunt Tillie huffed out an annoyed sound that was halfway between a furious cat growl and a rabid dog bark. "You're not the boss of me."

"No, but I have an FBI agent with me." I gestured toward Landon. "He can legally seize that gun."

"Actually, I can't do that," Landon countered, causing my insides to squirm. "Trust me, I've checked. She has that gun registered, and as long as she isn't taking off into the woods with the express purpose of hunting out of season or threatening someone, there's absolutely nothing I can do."

That was so not what I wanted to hear. "Whose side are you on?"

"I'm always on your side. That doesn't mean I can take that gun from her. Besides, you warned me before I left that I couldn't be Mr. FBI. You said I had to play by your rules. I'm here ... and I'm going to play by your rules."

"Oh, that should be a television show," Thistle teased. "*Mr. FBI*, where witches do all the heavy lifting and 'The Man' does absolutely nothing."

I glared holes into the side of her head. "Excuse me?"

"I like the sound of that." Aunt Tillie rested the butt of her gun on the ground and leaned against it. "As for Bessie here, she's coming with me. We have no idea what's in that barn. We might need to kill it."

Landon cocked his head. "Bessie? Since when did you name your gun?"

"She's always been Bessie."

"Not really," Thistle countered, shifting gears. "When we were kids you told us the gun's name was Aphrodite because we could kiss our rear ends goodbye if we didn't obey you."

Aunt Tillie snickered. "I forgot I told you that. You guys would believe anything."

"Ha, ha." I rolled my eyes. "You can't take the gun." I was adamant. "Something could happen. What if you accidentally kill one of the agents in Potter's Field because you're surprised?"

"Huh." Landon shifted from one foot to the other, clearly uncomfortable. "I didn't think about that. Maybe you should leave Bessie behind."

"No way." Aunt Tillie refused to back down. "Bessie is going. We're a team ... just like you and Bay are a team."

"I think there's a difference," Landon argued as the beams of Clove's headlights bounced against his face as she parked next to the Explorer. "I can't use Bay to accidentally kill someone in the woods."

"That's not true." Aunt Tillie refused to back down. "Bay is a stronger weapon than Bessie. You simply don't know how to load her correctly."

Landon slowly slid his eyes to me. "What's that supposed to mean?"

I shrugged. "No idea. Sometimes I think she talks simply to hear herself talk."

"What are you guys talking about?" Clove asked, appearing in front of her car. She looked nervous, as if this was the last place she wanted to be. "By the way, if I get eaten by an alien tonight I'll never forgive you guys."

"That seems fair," I said pragmatically.

"You're not going to be eaten by an alien." Aunt Tillie's tone was withering as she held up her gun. "I brought Bessie. She'll protect us. Have you learned nothing from all the movies I made you watch as kids? We'll be fine."

Clove wrinkled her forehead. "Bessie? I thought you named the gun Medusa because she was so ugly and terrible all your enemies turned to stone when you brandished her."

"Oh, geez." Aunt Tillie cursed under her breath. "You guys never forget anything. You're like elephants."

"We should get going," Landon interjected. "It's going to take a while to make it through the woods tonight. It's dark and we can't use flashlights. We should leave now."

"I have the flashlight problem taken care of," Aunt Tillie supplied, resting her shotgun against her shoulder as she marched toward the water. "Everything is under control. Trust me."

Landon flicked his eyes to me as he linked his fingers with mine. "I'm starting to think this was a terrible idea."

"You wanted to be part of the team," I reminded him.

"Our team." He gestured between the two of us. "You're my team."

"Yes, well, I come with ... auxiliary team members. I can't help it."

"We should've left Aunt Tillie behind." Landon sounded bitter. "If she shoots someone, we're going to be in real trouble."

"We might need her," I reminded him. "If there is an alien in that barn and it attacks, Aunt Tillie might be the only one who can stop it."

"Because of Bessie?"

"Because she's powerful."

Landon cocked an eyebrow. "You're powerful, too. That's why she made that crack about you being the most powerful weapon at my disposal."

I was uncomfortable with his scrutiny. "I don't want to be a weapon."

"I get that." Landon tucked a strand of hair behind my ear. "You're more than the sum of your parts. Remember that."

It was hard to forget. "Let's get moving. E.T. might be waiting."

"Or the predator," Aunt Tillie interjected, moving ahead of me to cross Hollow Creek first.

"Right. How could I forget about the predator?"

"I have no idea. You're embarrassing at the oddest of times."

THE WALK TO HANK'S HOUSE was difficult. Aunt Tillie conjured sentries of sorts, lighted spheres that illuminated the way through the forest. They were smaller than normal because we couldn't risk being seen. They looked like firefly swarms, which was disconcerting if you weren't a big fan of bugs.

"I knew this was a terrible idea." Clove swatted at a sentry buzzing close to her face. "I don't know why I let you guys talk me into these things. I hate it when you dream up adventures like this. I'm not the adventurous sort."

"How could you grow up in your family and not be adventurous?" Landon challenged. He kept close to my side, his eyes keen on the ground, but otherwise seemed calm. If I had to guess, the simple act of being proactive lessened some of the weight dragging him down. "I would think your childhood was nothing but an adventure."

"That's not a good thing," Clove shot back. "Adventures are stupid. I always wanted to play princess ... or Barbie dolls ... or even dress-up. Thistle and Bay never wanted that."

"That's not true," Thistle argued. "I liked playing dress-up."

"You always wanted to dress up like a monster ... or pretend to be Jason from the *Friday the 13th* movies."

"And that wasn't fun for you?" Thistle mocked surprise. "I'm shocked. Shocked, I tell you!"

Landon grinned as he squeezed my hand. "What did you like to dress up like, Bay?"

I shrugged, noncommittal. "I don't know. I don't really remember."

"She dressed up like Princess Leia," Thistle automatically answered. "Oh, and Captain Kirk. She was always a science fiction fan. That drove Clove crazy because she only identified with the princesses who needed a prince to run to the rescue."

"That is a lie!" Clove was incensed. "I don't need to be rescued."

"Then stop your bellyaching," Aunt Tillie barked. "I don't see why you guys have to be such kvetches. We're chasing aliens, for crying out loud. You can't whine when you're chasing aliens. Ripley would be so disappointed."

"Ripley?" Landon didn't bother to hide his amusement. "I take it that you think we're going to be fighting the sort of aliens who have acid for blood."

"I didn't say that." Aunt Tillie shook her free hand and dropped something on the ground. I narrowed my eyes and slowed my pace. The only reason I noticed what she was doing was because the sentries illuminated her frame at the right time.

"What was that?"

Aunt Tillie glanced from side to side. "What was what?"

"That." I pointed toward the spot where she'd dropped what she'd held in her hand. "You're throwing something on the ground as we walk."

Aunt Tillie drew herself up taller — which wasn't easy because she didn't clear five feet — and puffed out her chest. "I most certainly did not. You know how I feel about littering."

"I do, which is why I'm suspicious." I released Landon's hand and moved to where I saw her drop her load, squinting as I tried to make out what she'd dropped. Finally, I had no choice but to dig in my pocket for my cell phone. I held it up so I could use the screen as a flashlight and frowned as I knelt.

"What is it?" Landon appeared at my back and leaned over my shoulder. "What is that? I can't quite make it out."

I lifted one of the items in question and frowned. "It's a piece of candy."

"Reese's Pieces, right?" Thistle was amused. "I thought we were facing off with the predator, not E.T."

Aunt Tillie didn't look happy about being caught. "I didn't say it would be the predator, simply that we should prepare ourselves that it might be the predator. By the way, if we're assuming movie roles, I'm Arnold Schwarzenegger. I call dibs."

"Fine, then I'm the chick who never fires a gun and survives," I shot back. "Seriously, why are you dropping Reese's Pieces as we walk?"

Even though it was dark, the sentries made it impossible for Aunt Tillie to hide the flush creeping up her neck. "Maybe I simply have holes in my pockets. Did you ever consider that? My clothes are old."

"I happen to know those pants are new," Thistle argued. "I saw Mom and Marnie ordering them after the leggings debacle. They wanted to make sure that the dragons went extinct again."

Aunt Tillie rolled her eyes. "Oh, geez. I can't believe I'm related to such prudes."

"And I can't believe you're being so obvious." I dusted off my hands as I stood. "You're dropping the candy just in case E.T. is real, aren't you?"

"Of course not."

I waited.

"Fine." Aunt Tillie's eyes fired, promising retribution later. "I want to cover my bases. Sue me. If the alien is nice, I want to get a collar for him and train him as a pet."

"That sounds healthy," Landon muttered. "Seven witches and an alien. That sounds like a bad television show."

"Don't forget the crabby FBI agent who lives with them," I supplied sunnily.

Landon's lips curved up. "He's my favorite character."

"Mine, too."

"Okay, second favorite." He slung an arm around my shoulders and tugged me close to him. "The fifth witch is probably my favorite. She has a certain pizazz."

I was embarrassed to admit it — even to myself — but my insides went a little gooey. "She does have pizazz."

"Ugh. I'm totally going to vomit." Aunt Tillie made a face. "Can we get back to important things?"

"You mean the fact that you're trying to entice an alien to be your pet isn't important?" Thistle drawled. "I have trouble believing that."

"Keep it up, mouth," Aunt Tillie warned. "You've been off my list for a week. That can change."

"You said I was on your list a few days ago," Thistle countered. "Did you forget?"

Aunt Tillie was scandalized. "I would never forget something like that. You're simply low on the list because of all the FBI buttheads. There are a lot of them, so they take up pages of the list."

"Good to know." Thistle's eyes were keen as she scanned the thickening trees to our left. She held up one hand to still us. "We're here." Her voice was barely a whisper.

Everyone snapped to attention at her words, conversation ceasing.

Landon leaned so close his lips brushed the ridge of my ear, sending shivers down my spine. "Where?"

I pointed through the trees. "The barn is right there. Can you see the gleam on the door handle?"

Landon stared a long beat. "Yeah. That's where you think the alien is?"

"I didn't say it was an alien." He was trying my patience. "I merely said he was hiding something in his barn and it was suspect given the timing of the crash in the field."

"The flying saucer crash."

"Oh, don't turn condescending." My earlier adoration evaporated. "If you're going to be a pain, you can turn around right now and head back. I don't need this."

Landon held up his hands. "I'm sorry. I was simply trying to lighten the mood. It won't happen again."

Aunt Tillie tossed a handful of Reese's Pieces in Landon's direction, several pieces bouncing off his head as he glowered. "Shh. I'm in charge now."

"What makes you think you're in charge?" Thistle challenged.

"I'm the oldest."

"And I'm the smartest," Thistle fired back.

"And I'm the one with the training," Landon argued. "I'm going to head over there first. I want all of you to wait in the trees until I give you the all clear. Then you can approach."

I balked. "I didn't agree to that. You said you weren't going to turn into Mr. FBI."

"How is that turning into Mr. FBI? I'm simply trying to keep the people I love safe. You should be applauding me instead of attacking."

"Oh, listen to Mr. Condescending," Aunt Tillie trilled. "I can't believe you brought him, Bay. Have I taught you nothing?"

"Guys." Clove's voice was insistent as she stared at a spot over her shoulder. "Guys, you need to stop fighting."

"If we stop fighting, we'll have absolutely nothing to talk about," Thistle said. "That's going to make the walk back home really boring."

"Shut up," Clove hissed, her eyes flashing. "I ... you ... we ... ."

Right away, I realized something was wrong. "What is it?"

"Someone is over there." Clove extended a shaking finger. "I think it's a person ... or maybe an alien." Her lower lip trembled as she met my gaze. "We're not alone."

ALIEN INSPIRATION

> I wish *Men In Black* was real. I don't really care about the aliens, but I would love one of those big guns. Can you imagine the terror I could elicit from my enemies with that gun? Of course, I'm me. I don't need the gun to terrify people.
> **Aunt Tillie on science fiction weaponry**

SEVENTEEN

YOU'LL BELIEVE A WITCH CAN FLY!

The hair on the back of my neck stood on end as the sound of footsteps assailed my ears.

Landon reacted quickly, grabbing my arm and jerking me behind him so he could stand as a shield.

I didn't believe it was an alien, not from that direction. The other option simply made more sense. It seemed Agent Gibson's men had finally caught up with us. I pictured myself being locked in a tiny cell with no windows, being cut off from those I loved as the government locked me away for the rest of my life. Being separated from Aunt Tillie, my mother and aunts wasn't so terrible. I would miss Landon, Thistle and Clove, though.

That was not how I wanted to go down, but I was frozen in fear and couldn't make my legs work.

Then I heard voices ... and not the voices I'd expected.

"Watch where you're going, Jace. You almost tripped me."

"I didn't almost trip you."

"You did so. We're supposed to be professionals. You're not acting like a professional."

The oxygen trapped in my lungs escaped in a low hiss as I relaxed.

AMANDA M. LEE

At the same moment, Ryan, Morgan and Jace stumbled into the small clearing where I stood, making for a less-than-graceful entrance. Their eyes all went wide when they realized they weren't alone.

"Who goes there?" Ryan barked.

Landon rolled his eyes as he relaxed. "Oh, geez. Let me guess. These are the alien hunters you were hanging around with this afternoon.?"

I bobbed my head. "Yup."

"Who are you?" Jace's eyes narrowed when he saw Landon's arm around my waist. "Are you an alien?"

Landon's irritation was on full display. "Why would you think I'm an alien?"

"Because chicks can't stay away from aliens. Haven't you seen *Thor* ... and *Roswell* ... and *Starman* ... oh, and *Superman*? He's the biggest alien of all. Women love aliens."

I scratched my head. "Um ... ."

"I'm with the FBI," Landon challenged. "I'm not an alien."

"You're not exactly making your case there, Skippy," Aunt Tillie interjected when the three younger men shrank back. "I'm sure aliens are better than Feds as far as they're concerned."

"We have a right to be here." Ryan squared his shoulders as he held Landon's gaze. "We've broken no laws and we know our rights. If you try to take us into custody we'll ... well, we know our rights."

"He's not going to take you into custody." I was almost positive that was true. "Don't get all weird and stuff. That's the last thing we need."

Jace found his voice. "If he's not here to take us into custody, why is he here?"

"He's Bay's boyfriend." Thistle was smug as she delivered the news. "They live together. He decided to tag along for tonight's excursion to make sure we were safe."

Jace didn't hide the fact that he was crestfallen very well. "You have a boyfriend? I ... why didn't you tell me you had a boyfriend?"

I was taken aback. "I didn't think it was necessary."

"Oh, really?" Jace's eyes fired with something I couldn't quite identify. "You didn't think it was important to tell me you had a boyfriend? What about all those sparks flying earlier between us?" He gestured wildly, his finger pointing at me and then himself multiple times. "How can you have a boyfriend when we sparked the way we did?"

Landon arched a challenging eyebrow as he slid me a sidelong look. "Is there something you want to tell me?"

Becoming defensive was the wrong move, but I couldn't stop myself. "There were no sparks."

"Oh, there were sparks," Jace snapped. "There were sparks everywhere. I burned all over."

I bit my lip to keep from laughing. The situation wasn't funny, but his reaction was so surreal it bordered on hilarious. "You burned all over?"

"I think he means in his nether regions," Clove offered helpfully. "He's saying his loins were burning for you."

Jace's mouth dropped open. "I don't have burning loins."

"Oh, geez." Landon ruefully rubbed his forehead. "This night couldn't get any worse."

"It could totally get worse," Thistle argued as Aunt Tillie threw another handful of candy at Landon's face. "Trust me."

I sucked in a calming breath and held up my hands. "I think we're getting off on a tangent here. It doesn't matter who had burning loins or who thought it was a simply an innocent excursion into the woods …."

Jace cut me off. "I don't have burning loins!"

Landon chuckled, the sound low and throaty. "I love going on adventures with you, sweetie. Have I ever told you that?"

I ignored the hint of sarcasm in his voice. "We need to focus on the task at hand," I reminded everyone. "We're all here to see what's in that barn. Can't we all work together until we succeed and then argue about burning loins later?"

Jace jutted out his lower lip and folded his arms across his chest. "I don't think I'm comfortable working with the Feds."

"Join the club," Aunt Tillie drawled. "You'll have to get used to it. This one won't go anywhere without her pet agent." She pointed at me. "And he definitely won't leave her to investigate an alien in a barn. He's all alpha and stuff, likes to show off his muscles."

Landon made a face. "I do not."

"You do." Aunt Tillie refused to back down. "I've seen you shirtless so many times I've wondered if the guesthouse suddenly turned into a *Baywatch* convention."

Offended, Landon growled. "I don't walk around shirtless anywhere except in the privacy of my own home. Have you ever considered that the only reason you see me shirtless so often is because you let yourself into our bedroom without knocking?"

"No."

Jace's misery continued to mount. "You guys live together?"

"I believe I already mentioned that," Thistle supplied. "Keep up."

"But ... what about the spark?"

Landon extended a warning finger. "Stop talking about the spark. There was no spark."

"You weren't there," Jace persisted. "There was a spark." He looked to his comrades for confirmation. "Tell him about the spark."

"I don't know, dude." Morgan shifted from one foot to the other, uncomfortable about being put on the spot. "You said there was a spark, but she just seemed like a nice old lady. I don't think there was a spark."

Now it was my turn to be offended. "Old lady? Who are you calling old?"

"It's not so much fun when the shoe is on the other foot, is it?" Aunt Tillie looked smug. "That will teach you to call me old."

"I rarely call you old," I fired back. "You have me confused with Thistle."

"I do call you old," Thistle agreed readily. "I think memory loss is a sign of age, so you're not really helping your argument."

"You're definitely on my list now," Aunt Tillie snapped.

"I am not old," I repeated. "I'm young. I'm in my prime."

"You are, sweetie." Landon absently patted my shoulder as he focused on the barn. "So I believe we'd just agreed that I was going to check out the barn on my own before we were so rudely interrupted. Let's go back to that plan."

"You're not going alone." I was firm as I turned to Morgan. "I am not old."

"You remind me of my mom," Morgan argued. "She's like you."

"Ugh." I pressed my eyes shut to gather my patience. "I hate this day. I mean ... hate it. It's the stupidest day ever."

"Bay, don't get yourself worked up," Landon chided. "I like older women. Ask me about my Michelle Pfeiffer obsession. It's a thing."

Thistle snorted at my outraged expression. "I don't think you're doing yourself any favors, Landon."

"Definitely not," Clove agreed. "As for the barn, I've changed my mind. I no longer want to see what's inside. I think we should abandon this plan and go for doughnuts and ice cream. I'm craving doughnuts and ice cream for some reason."

"You've been craving doughnuts and ice cream all week," Thistle countered. "It's getting ridiculous. We're heading into bathing suit season. You need to cut down on the carbs ... and sugar ... and the fat, for that matter, or you're going to be shopping in the one-piece section this year."

Clove's gaze was hot. "That's the meanest thing you've ever said to me."

"You'll get over it."

Landon snapped his fingers to get everyone's attention. "I am not kidding. I didn't hike all the way out here to spend the entire night having an argument about bathing suits and sparks. We need to keep our eyes on the prize."

"That was an inspired speech," Aunt Tillie deadpanned. "Seriously, it was straight out of *Rocky*."

"You know what? You're on my list." Landon's temper came out to play. "How do you like that? You're at the very top."

Aunt Tillie merely shrugged. "If you're going to do something, you might as well do it right. I'm happy to be at the top of your list, although I have a feeling I won't stay long given the way that pouty guy keeps looking at Bay's butt when he thinks you're not looking."

AMANDA M. LEE

Landon snapped his eyes back to Jace. "Don't make me thump you."

"I wasn't doing anything." Jace's voice turned whiny. "We had a spark. It was a genuine spark."

"Shut up about the spark." Landon turned bossy. "If you mention the imaginary spark again, we're going to fight. Do you want to fight me?"

"No."

"Then shut it." Landon shook his head and leveled his gaze at the barn. "Okay, here's what we're going to do."

"THIS WAS NOT THE PLAN."

Landon glared at Aunt Tillie as she paused in front of the barn door and rested her hands on the padlock that separated us from what was inside.

"Suck it up, Whinebox," Aunt Tillie snapped. "You need me to get inside ... and to serve as backup should the predator jump out and try to skin you alive."

"Uh-huh." Landon was clearly unconvinced when he shifted his eyes to me. "And why are you here?"

"Because it was my idea and I have to see what's in there for myself," I replied without hesitation. "You said you weren't going to be Mr. FBI."

"I said that before I saw the creepy barn you guys wanted to break into. Now I want to make sure you don't touch anything rusty that requires a tetanus shot. That would put a crimp in my plans for tonight."

Something occurred to me. "You only wanted to come tonight because of the romance factor, didn't you?"

"No. I won't deny that you get all riled up after adventurous outings in the middle of the night, but that's not the only reason I came. I wasn't lying when I said I missed working with you."

"Oh, well, that's kind of sweet."

"You're such an easy mark," Aunt Tillie complained. "Why must you be such an easy mark? I didn't teach you to be that way."

"I guess I must have figured it out on my own," I said dryly. "You should be treating me like a queen right now, by the way. I'm the one who talked Thistle and Clove into staying in the bushes with the alien-hunting trio. That'll make it easier for us to get in and out of this barn."

"I arranged that," Landon corrected. "I had to flash my badge and everything. I figured it was our one shot at seeing what was inside this place."

"Yes, well, I still played a part in it," I grumbled.

"Of course you did." Landon gave me a quick kiss on the cheek before focusing on Aunt Tillie. "Are you going to open that door?"

"I am." Aunt Tillie's fingers pulsed with energy as she whispered a spell that caused the lock to tumble. She jerked to open it and then removed the chain. "See. I've got everything under control."

"That's another reason I want those guys staying behind," Landon added. "If you guys need to do something witchy, I don't want them writing about it on their blog."

That was a fair point. "I think they're going to be writing about sparks of a different sort for the next week or so."

Landon scowled. "If you mention the sparks again, we're going to fight."

"Fine."

"Both of you need to shut up," Aunt Tillie ordered, throwing open the double doors and peering into the darkness. "We're here to find the alien, not argue about your boring love life."

"Our love life isn't boring," Landon shot back. "Also, I'm not here looking for an alien. I'm simply here because I'm worried that this Hank person has someone chained in his barn."

I tilted my head, considering. "When did that become your primary concern?"

"It was always my primary concern."

"You never mentioned it."

"Well, I'm mentioning it now." Landon stepped closer to the opening and frowned. "It's pitch black in here. Where is the light?"

"There is no light," I replied. "I told you, he doesn't have electricity."

"That's why this barn makes sense to hide the alien," Aunt Tillie said sagely. "Aliens can do things with electricity — you know, like Magneto can with metal — so it's best to lock them in places without electricity."

"What movie did you see that in?" I challenged. "I've never seen that."

"*Stranger Things.*"

I racked my brain. "First, those aren't aliens. They're from the Upside Down, and it's a different thing entirely. Secondly, Eleven is the one who can blow up electrical gadgets, and she's human."

"Are you telling me how to interpret my favorite television show ever?" Aunt Tillie challenged.

"*The Walking Dead* is your favorite television show. Even though it sucks these days, you still watch it religiously."

"That's because Daryl is my spirit animal."

"I thought Tonya Harding was your spirit animal," I argued. "That's what you said after watching *I, Tonya.*"

"She is. I'm both Daryl and Tonya. I can be both things."

"Shh," Landon admonished as he took a step into the barn. We both ignored him.

"I think you just like being difficult," I shot back. "There's no alien out here." The longer we stood and talked about it, the more foolish I felt. "I'm on Landon's side. It's probably some poor woman Hank found at a bus stop. He probably has her chained in here, and we're going to be heroes when we save her."

"Be quiet," Landon ordered.

"It's an alien," Aunt Tillie insisted. "I'm telling you ... things are about to go very *Third Rock from the Sun.*"

Hmm. "Does that mean we're going to feel like idiots when this is over?"

"Very possibly."

"Shut up!" Landon's voice whipped out, cruising past agitation and banking at fury. "I'm not kidding."

Aunt Tillie glared at him. "Well, I never."

"Don't you hear that?" Landon persisted, crouching a bit so he could make out the sound. "There's something in here."

"We told you that already," Aunt Tillie said. "Didn't you believe us?"

"I ... ." Landon worked his jaw, but no sound came out. He was intent enough that I forced myself to abandon the argument with Aunt Tillie and focus on the barn.

"I don't hear anything," I said after a beat. "In fact ... ." I trailed off when I realized Landon was right. There was definitely something in the barn. I heard something dragging across the packed earth of the floor. It sounded like something with multiple legs ... or arms ... or tentacles.

My mouth went dry. "What is that?"

"I don't know," Landon hissed. "I wish I had thought to bring a flashlight."

"We agreed it was a bad idea in case the agents in the field saw it," I reminded him.

"Yes, but we can't see anything right now and I would rather deal with agents than the unknown."

He had a point. "Well, we could ... ." I didn't get a chance to finish because Aunt Tillie decided to take control of the situation.

"I've got this." She waved her hand in the air at the exact moment I realized what she was going to do.

"No. Wait!"

It was too late. The sentries that had scattered when we'd stumbled across Jace and his crew regrouped and swarmed as they barreled past us into the barn, a thousand buzzing lights illuminating the barn. My eyes widened when I caught a hint of movement ... and then I saw a set of glowing eyes, along with razor-sharp teeth.

"Oh, my ... Goddess!"

"What is that?" Landon sounded unnaturally shrill as he grabbed my arm and attempted to pull me from the barn. "Holy ... get away from it now! Don't look at it!"

"It's an alien." Aunt Tillie was in awe. "Finally! I'm going to teach it to do tricks and open wormholes in my closet!"

"You're not doing anything of the sort!" Landon gave Aunt Tillie a shove. "You need to start moving. Run!"

It was too late. The thing in the barn had already seen us. We were now its focus. Running couldn't save us.

ALIEN INSPIRATION

> How come the aliens in these movies always want to kill first and ask questions later? I'm a witty conversationalist. They should give it a shot. Just think of all the good times we could have with a cup of tea and a *Keeping Up With the Kardashians* marathon.
> **Twila ruins *Alien* for her family**

EIGHTEEN

A NEW KIND OF ENEMY. A NEW KIND OF WITCH.

I registered three things in rapid succession.

Whatever was in the barn had gleaming fangs.

Aunt Tillie was raising her shotgun.

Oh, and Landon was trying to shove me out of the barn to get me away from the attack while standing as a rather enticing target.

I ignored all those things, however, and stood my ground.

"Don't." I fought Landon's efforts and shook my head. "I'm fine."

Landon's eyes widened. "You're fine? There's some ... rabid creature in there that could eat you. You're not fine."

I refused to rise to his provocation and freak out for no good reason. "And it hasn't attacked, in case you haven't noticed." I slapped Aunt Tillie's arm to get her to lower the gun. "Don't shoot. It's Foxy Carmichael."

Aunt Tillie stared for a long moment, the butt of the shotgun resting against her shoulder. Finally, she slid her gaze to me and frowned. "How can you be sure?"

"Because I stole her," Hank announced, moving into the barn behind us. He didn't appear surprised to see us. In fact, he looked more resigned than anything else as he crossed the barn and knelt next to the huge dog sitting in the middle of the space. The mutt looked like a mix between a St. Bernard and a standard poodle, with a few out-of-control hair issues to top off the rather odd genetic combination. "She's not dangerous. You just startled her."

"Wait a second." Landon held up his hands and glanced around. "What is going on here? Who is Foxy Carmichael?"

"The dog," I explained. "She belongs to Roger Nelson ... except he doesn't take care of her. She's famous around town because she runs ... and begs ... and occasionally steals. Nelson doesn't feed her, so she visits various houses."

"Holy crap!" Thistle moved into the barn and shook her head as she stared at the dog. "I thought maybe something happened to her. Marcus feeds her every day — and he's been making noise about offering Roger money for her. He'll be glad to hear she's alive."

"I still don't understand," Landon pressed. "Who names a dog Foxy Carmichael?"

"That's what you're worried about?" Thistle graced Landon with a derisive look as she circled him and approached Hank. The prepper was on his knees, stroking the dog and cooing calming words in her ear. "Can I take a look, Hank?"

Hank nodded as he watched her move closer to the dog. "I knew you guys would be back. You heard Foxy and you couldn't let it go. Are you going to take her back to Roger?"

"Absolutely not." Thistle was firm as she shook her head and used her illuminated phone screen to study the dog's paw more closely. "She needs to go to a vet, Hank. She's a good dog and everyone loves her for a reason. If you're going to keep her, you have to take care of her ... and that includes going to the vet."

"That means going into town," I prodded. "You're not much for going to town — and I get it — but when you take on an animal you take on the responsibility for taking care of that animal."

Landon's mouth dropped open as his gaze bounced between faces. He was so flabbergasted he barely looked up when Clove and the three alien hunters joined us. "You can't just help him keep a stolen dog."

"Roger Nelson is a jerk," I countered. "He doesn't take care of Foxy. The town takes care of her. She comes out to the inn and Mom feeds her once a week. The dog has a rotation, but she deserves someone to take care of her."

"I don't disagree, but this guy lives in the woods without electricity and running water."

"So what?" Out of all Hank's peculiarities, that bothered me least. "He takes care of himself, has a wood-burning stove and he has plenty of food. I mean ... do they make prepper dog food, Hank?"

"They do, and I've already ordered it." Hank's gaze was dark when it landed on Landon. "I'll take care of her."

"But ... what about her owner?"

"Roger Nelson is an ass," Aunt Tillie explained, resting the butt of her gun on the floor and shaking her head as she watched Hank dote on Foxy. "You really should have told me what was going on, Hank. I could've helped you."

"How could you have helped him?" Thistle asked.

Aunt Tillie's smile was benign. "I have my ways."

"I have no doubt about that," Landon muttered, roughly scratching the back of his neck as he shook his head. "At least you guys can let the alien angle go now. I told you there were no such things as aliens."

Hank sobered. "Oh, aliens are real." He was solemn as he rested his hands on his knees and stared into Landon's eyes. "I've seen them ... and they're here."

"Uh-huh." Landon didn't look convinced. "Are we done? I want to go home and take a bath."

"We're not done here," Jace finally found his voice, although the expression on his face when looking at the dog didn't reflect nearly as much affection as the rest of us felt. "Has anyone considered that maybe this man put a pilfered dog on display because he knew we were coming and thought the dog would distract us?"

"Not really," Thistle said dryly. "People have been looking for this dog for days. Isn't that right, Foxy?" Thistle made a goofy face as she hugged the dog. "I'm so glad you're okay."

Landon watched Thistle with dumbfounded confusion. "I didn't realize she was a dog person."

"We had a dog," I volunteered. "She was awesome. She died a few years ago. She lived to be a ripe old age ... and then passed in her sleep."

"Even Aunt Tillie liked Sugar," Clove added. "She was the best dog."

"We spoiled her rotten," Thistle agreed.

Landon rubbed his cheek as he watched my surly cousin make kissing noises at the huge animal. "Why don't any of you have dogs now if you love them so much?"

"Aunt Tillie said no more dogs," Thistle replied. "Everyone was crushed when Sugar died, so ... no more dogs."

"I know it's hard to lose a pet, but ... not loving another animal seems a bad way to honor something that you really loved," Landon noted. "We'll talk about that when we get a chance.

"For now, I think it's clear that Hank wasn't really hiding an alien in his barn," he continued. "He has a dog — which you guys seem fine with him stealing — so we don't have to worry about anything else, right?"

"If I had an alien, trust me, you wouldn't suspect me of having an alien," Hank offered. "I would be much better at hiding it. Foxy needs attention. She can't stay in the barn forever. I want her to be able to enjoy the woods, but I can't with those jerks hanging around Potter's Field."

I stilled, surprised. "They're not still there, are they?"

Hank nodded. "That's where I was before you guys showed up. I heard them out there and wanted to see what they were doing. I knew you'd come, but I thought it would be later."

"Aunt Tillie turns into a pumpkin if she's not home in time for Jimmy Kimmel," Thistle offered.

Hank's face was blank. "I'll take your word for it."

"He doesn't have a television," Clove reminded Thistle. "He has no idea who Jimmy Kimmel is."

"This is why I'm not looking forward to the end of the world," Thistle complained. "How am I supposed to survive the apocalypse if I don't have Netflix to unwind with?"

She had a point. Of course, I was too busy dwelling on Hank's words to give it much thought. "How many people are out in that field, Hank?"

"Very few now," Hank answered. "I think they're finishing up."

"Did you see what they were doing?" Landon asked, taking me by surprise. "Did you ever see them remove anything big from the site?"

"Like a flying saucer?" Jace prodded.

Hank shook his head. "I think whatever was out there was dragged away that first night. I heard heavy trucks on the highway. And they shut it down so no one but federal employees could drive on the roadway. After that, they kept searching for something, but I don't think they ever found the alien they were looking for."

Landon bit back a sigh, but barely. "How do you know they were looking for an alien?"

Hank shrugged, noncommittal. "What else would they be looking for?"

"Maybe there was something on the craft when it crashed," Landon suggested. "Maybe there was a weapon they didn't want anyone to find out about ... or some kind of poison that can hurt crops or people. Have you ever considered that?"

I nodded without hesitation. "That was my initial guess."

"And?"

I shrugged. "I don't know. That got boring after a bit. It was more fun to think there were aliens running around."

"I always thought aliens were a possibility," Clove said. "I have a mind as open as my heart."

"You have a mind as small as Mrs. Little's imagination," Thistle corrected. "I told you aliens were never a possibility."

"If you didn't believe aliens were a possibility, what are you doing out here?" Ryan challenged.

"Someone needed to serve as a chaperone," Thistle replied. "With Landon going over the edge, I was the only sane one left."

"Hey! I didn't go over the edge." Landon extended a warning finger. "I never believed it was aliens."

"Then why are you out here?" Jace challenged. "I'll tell you why you're out here. You're trying to smother our spark." He sent me a winning smile. "Don't fall for his act. He doesn't have your best interests at heart."

"I'm going to have to start smacking him around," Landon shook his head. "Seriously, I can't hear another word about the spark."

"Forget the spark," I instructed, my temper flaring. "We have other things to worry about."

"We do?" Landon knit his eyebrows. "What are we worrying about?"

"The field," I answered without hesitation. "This is probably the last night they'll be out there."

Landon's bored expression didn't waver. "So what?"

"So this is our last chance to figure out what they're up to," I pressed. "Once they're gone, that's it. We'll never know what they're hiding."

"What if they're not hiding anything?" Landon asked. "What if this is all in your head?"

I wasn't ruling out that possibility, but it wasn't something I wanted to dwell on. "I have to see. Up until about five minutes ago, you had to see, too."

"That was before I broke into a barn to find an alien that turned out to be a dog."

"Then stay here." I was serious as we snagged gazes. "You should stay here with Jace, Ryan and Morgan. The rest of us will hit the field and report back on what we find."

"No way." Jace vehemently shook his head. "I am not being left behind. We have a right to know what's out there."

"We want to believe," Morgan intoned, causing me to roll my eyes.

"Then Landon, you can stay here with Hank and help him take care of Foxy," I suggested. "We won't be gone long. When we get back, we can cross the creek together and head home to take a bath."

"Don't forget, you're responsible for getting Aunt Tillie home,"

Thistle prodded. "I'm not taking her with me. If you don't drive her she'll be stuck out here and we might never see her again if she can't find her way home. I'd be fine with that, but our mothers are a different story."

"We've got Aunt Tillie under control," Landon supplied.

"Famous last words," I muttered under my breath, collecting myself. "I still have to go to Potter's Field. I know you don't want to and it's fine if you stay here. I won't be gone long."

Landon rolled his eyes. "Right. Like I'm going to just sit here while you wander off into the dark with spark boy." He openly glared at Jace. "I'm going with you."

"Well, then stop complaining." I wiped my hands on my jeans as I focused on Aunt Tillie. "I know you don't want to hear this, but it might be smart for you to stay here until we get back."

"That's not going to happen." Aunt Tillie's eyes fired. "I'm going with you. I want to see the alien."

"There is no alien," Landon barked.

Aunt Tillie ignored him. "Besides, Bay, you might need me if you try to communicate with a being from another planet. I'm the only one who can speak alien."

"I don't think alien is a dialect," Thistle pointed out.

"And I don't think I'm talking to you," Aunt Tillie shot back. "I'll have you know ... I speak Klingon."

"She does," Clove agreed sagely. "I've heard her. She waits for Worf to say something on reruns of *Star Trek: The Next Generation* and then she repeats the words."

"I can still speak it," Aunt Tillie complained.

"Who cares?" Landon was clearly at his wit's end as he shook his head. "From what I can gather, everyone insists on seeing the field. I think it's a bad idea, but I'm not letting you out of my sight, Bay. Apparently, we're all doing this together."

"That's because he wants to smother our spark," Jace whispered.

"I am going to start smacking you around if you don't shut your mouth," Landon warned. "I'm feeling aggressive. I think it might make me feel better if I hurt you."

Jace puffed out his chest. "I'm not afraid of you."

"Then you're dumber than you look, sparky." Aunt Tillie inclined her chin toward the barn door. "If we're going to go, now's the time."

"Then let's go." Landon held out his hand for me. "If we all get arrested I'm blaming everyone with the last name of Winchester."

Clove balked. "What did I do?"

"You get them all worked up," Landon answered. "And you enjoy it."

"I think you're exaggerating," Clove sniffed. "I'm the good one."

"That's not saying much." Landon gripped my hand. "Let's move. I want this night to be over. If we're lucky, Gibson will be out of here tomorrow and I'll have my turf back. I'm sick of not being in charge."

"Let's go," I agreed. "I want it done with, too."

LANDON MADE SURE TO keep Jace and his buddies far to our right as we crept toward Potter's Field. He explained during the short walk that he thought it was a good idea because we would be less likely to be seen by Gibson's men if we broke into smaller groups, but I had no doubt why he really wanted to divide the groups: His nose was out of joint.

"Are you really jealous of Jace?" I asked him in a low voice as we picked our way through the trees.

"I don't get jealous."

"Of course. What was I thinking?" I bit back a smirk. "A cool guy like you would never get jealous. I must have been imagining the way you reacted to Jace."

"I am not jealous of that guy," Landon persisted.

"I never said you were."

We lapsed into silence for a while before Landon felt the urge to break it. "Maybe I was a little jealous. It wasn't a lot, though, so I don't feel it's necessary for you to comment on it."

"Of course not." I pressed my lips together to keep from laughing. "I appreciate it, just for the record."

"You appreciate what?"

"The fact that you're jealous. It bolsters my ego."

Landon sighed. "You make it impossible to be irritated with you sometimes. You know that, right?"

"That's what I'm going for."

"Well, you're succeeding. In fact ... ." Landon trailed off when a noise in front of us caught his attention. He held up his hand to still everyone — mimicking a scene right out of *Predator*, although I wasn't sure he realized he was doing it — but no one other than Aunt Tillie and me stopped. He looked pained when everyone kept going. "We need to stop them."

"I think it's too late for that," Aunt Tillie said, cocking her head to the side as her eyes shifted to the sky. "I think it's too late for all of us."

My inner danger alarm tripped at the same time she said the last word. I jerked my head to the right, sensing movement before I actually saw it. This time I was certain that the shifting shadows didn't belong to anyone from our group.

"Run," I hissed, giving Landon a good shove. "Don't let them take you. We'll take care of ourselves. You could lose your job."

"Yes, run," Aunt Tillie agreed, her fingers flexing. "If you're not free and clear no one will be available to bail us out. You have no choice. Seriously ... run!"

ALIEN INSPIRATION

> If I had an alien I would want the one from *E.T. the Extraterrestrial*. He liked dressing up like a little old lady. Who doesn't love that? That's so much better than the ones that try to eat you.
>
> **Twila explaining her alien preferences**

NINETEEN

IF IT BLEEDS, SHE CAN KILL IT.

I don't know why I expected Landon to run. I couldn't see the expression on his face thanks to the darkness — Aunt Tillie doused the sentries before resuming our walk — but his body language told me he was having none of it.

"Don't be ridiculous," Landon hissed. "We're all going back together."

A blinding light hit me directly in the face. I shielded my eyes from the brightness and slouched as voices started barking out orders.

"Freeze."

"Stop right where you are."

"If you run, we'll shoot."

Aunt Tillie glared into the light, defiant. "Well, I guess that means we're not going to make it to the field."

"Oh, really?" Thistle asked dryly, raising her hands as an armed agent hurried to her side. "What was your first clue?"

"It'll be okay." Never one to back down, Aunt Tillie refused to relinquish her gun when another agent attempted to lighten her load. "Let me do the talking."

That sounded like a horrible idea. I slid a sidelong look to Landon, worry overtaking me. He didn't appear particularly perturbed about our predicament, though he was a master at hiding his emotions when the scenario called for it.

"Let Aunt Tillie do the talking," he suggested. "I think that's a great idea."

Yup. The world was surely coming to an end.

THEY TRANSPORTED US TO the police station, which buzzed with activity as we were shown inside. They didn't cuff us, which was a small comfort, but I figured that was probably because they didn't have enough cuffs to handle our entire group.

Agent Gibson was waiting in the conference room. He seemed full of himself — and then some — as his gaze shifted from one face to another before finally landing on Landon. "I expected you to pull a boneheaded move like this."

Landon shrugged. "I'm glad things worked out as you thought they would."

"You're in big trouble."

"I figured." Landon pulled out a chair so I could sit next to him. He appeared calm, stoic even, but I could sense the turmoil cascading through him. He was trying to figure a way out of this, although I wasn't certain that was possible.

"We insist on legal representation," I said once I was seated. "You can't hold us without providing lawyers."

"That's not true." Gibson sat across from me, smugness practically rolling off him in waves. "I'm not bound by state laws."

I didn't like the sound of that. "Well, that's ... awesome."

Landon rested his hand on top of mine. "Calm down, Bay. It's going to be okay."

"It is," Aunt Tillie agreed. She took the spot at the head of the table, her favorite power position, and kicked back in her chair as she regarded Gibson (who claimed the power position at the other end of the table). It was like a scene from a mob movie, with the two heads of the rival families finally facing off. "This guy can't hold us, and he knows it."

"I think you'll find that you're wrong there," Gibson countered. "I'm a federal agent. I can do anything."

"Is that true?" Clove's eyes widened as she turned to Landon. Her skin was an ashy color and she was taking on a green tinge that worried me. "Can he lock us up and throw away the key? Oh, is it going to be like *The Shawshank Redemption?*"

"In your case, I think it's going to be more *Orange is the New Black*," Thistle offered. "As long as you're willing to be someone's prison girlfriend, you'll be fine."

"Oh, I don't want to be a prison girlfriend," Clove lamented. "This is just the worst thing ever."

"Knock it off." Landon refused to panic. "No one is going to need a prison girlfriend."

"That's good." I had no idea why I continued to talk other than that my nerves were getting the better of me. "I don't think I would do well if that were the case. I can barely be your girlfriend without freaking out."

Landon chuckled, the sound low and throaty. "You'll be fine. Agent Gibson is simply posturing. He can't keep us."

Gibson's eyes gleamed with overt dislike. "You've been a problem from the start, Agent Michaels. You act as if you know everything ... and yet you know nothing."

"I know enough to recognize that you can't hold us," Landon pointed out. "You nabbed us on private land. It wasn't township land, no matter what you think. It was Hank William Jenkins' property, and I'm certain he didn't call you to ask for assistance. You have no jurisdiction to take us into custody on that land."

For the first time since we'd entered the room, Gibson looked slightly nervous. "No, you were on Hemlock Cove land ... and it was clearly marked off limits."

"Actually, it wasn't," Landon countered. "I told you to put tape up from every angle, but you insisted no one could enter from the west, so you didn't bother. That area wasn't marked."

Gibson worked his jaw. "I ... ."

"He's right," Thistle said after a beat. "We didn't see any tape or warnings."

"They're on the road," Ryan offered. "We saw them when we came to town. We tried to walk around the property, but couldn't find a place to enter that wasn't taped off. That's the only reason we went with you. There were no warnings from the direction we approached."

"That's because Agent Gibson didn't believe anyone could approach from the west," Landon explained. "He was certain that it wasn't possible ... so essentially he fell down on the job."

Gibson was livid as he slowly pushed himself to a standing position. "Agent Michaels, I think we should take this conversation into the hallway."

Landon didn't so much as shift in his chair. "I'm good here."

"We need to talk." Gibson was persistent. "I think you'll agree that it's better for you if we talk outside."

Even though he was stubborn by nature, I felt Landon's determination waning. He cast me a sidelong look, as if asking what I thought.

"You should probably go with him," I said finally. "He might really have something important to say." And he might offer Landon a deal that would save his job, I silently added.

Landon heaved out a sigh. "Fine." He didn't look happy when he stood. "Let's take this into the hallway." He leaned down to whisper in my ear. "Don't say anything while I'm gone. If someone tries to get you to admit something, don't. I'll be back as soon as I can."

I nodded and watched as Landon and Gibson filed out of the room. The second the door was shut, Aunt Tillie made a derogatory noise in the back of her throat.

"Good grief," she complained, waving her hand in front of her face. "Did anyone else think they were going to whip them out and start measuring?"

I glared at her, frustration bubbling up. "Landon could be in real trouble here. I think you should cut him some slack."

"Don't worry about Landon." Aunt Tillie flicked her eyes to the agent standing in the corner of the room. He was young and looked unsure of himself. "He'll be fine. For that matter, don't worry about us. I have everything under control."

That was a frightening thought. "You have everything under control?" The challenge came out shriller than I wanted. "How do you figure that? We're in FBI custody."

"Technically we're not," Thistle countered. "Sure, they insisted we leave the woods and ride with them into town — which I think we probably could've avoided if we had put up a fight — but they haven't read us our rights. I don't think we're in custody."

Hmm. That was an interesting notion. I hadn't really considered it. I was generally cool under pressure — er, well, at least compared to my relatives — but I was a ball of nerves waiting for Landon to return. "What do you think they're going to do to us?"

"They're probably going to hand us over to the aliens," Morgan replied calmly. "That's how things like this usually work."

My forehead wrinkled as I pondered the statement. "Excuse me? I'm not sure I understand."

"This always happens," Ryan volunteered. "Aliens land, the government covers it up, then those who fight the government disappear. Why? We're pretty sure the government comes to an agreement with the aliens and allows them to eat certain people. We'll probably be the first on the menu."

That was the most ridiculous thing I'd ever heard ... and I spent years sharing a roof with Aunt Tillie, the Queen of Ridiculous Thinking. "I don't think they're going to allow aliens to eat us," I said. "Don't worry about that."

"Oh, I'm not worried." Morgan was blasé. "I smoked pot before we hit the woods. I should be fine for another hour or so. Then I'll begin to worry."

"You smoked pot, huh?" I didn't want to laugh. It wasn't a funny situation. "Well, at least you've got that going for you."

"Where did you find the pot?" Aunt Tillie challenged. "Did you bring it with you or swipe from fields locally?"

Morgan didn't seem to understand the question. "What?"

"Ignore him." Jace rested his hands on the table and leaned forward, staring directly into my eyes. "I won't allow the aliens to eat you. I'll sacrifice myself to make sure it doesn't happen. I won't abandon you like your boyfriend."

"Landon didn't abandon me," I argued. "He's in the hallway."

"So you think." Jace wasn't about to be deterred. "You think he's out there, but he's really being removed from the situation because the government believes he's a threat. Right now he's probably serving as the first meal for our alien friends." He turned solemn. "I'm sorry for your loss."

Oh, geez. I couldn't wait to get away from these geeks. "Something tells me he'll be okay."

"I'm still sorry for your loss." Jace appeared sincere. "Once you're done mourning, we can revisit the spark ... that is if I haven't sacrificed myself to save you. It's okay to cry."

I rubbed my forehead as I snagged Thistle's gaze. "We should've headed home after the ridiculous scene at Hank's house," I groused. "I could be sitting in a warm bathtub right now."

"Yes, well, live and learn." Thistle focused on the light above the table. It was harsh and washed out everyone's features. "I think I'm going to give up trying to get Marcus to accept the statue."

"What statue?" She was going off on a tangent and I was having trouble keeping up.

"The naked one I told you about."

"Oh, right. The witch." I pursed my lips. "I forgot about that thanks to everything that happened. I still want to see it."

"Marcus put a blanket over it and hid it in the stable. He's embarrassed."

"Or he's simply afraid of being arrested for public indecency," I countered. "Think about it from his point of view. He's trying to entice families with children to come to the stables. They won't if you put a naked woman in front of the barn."

"I wanted to put it in our house."

"Maybe he's afraid that he'll become attracted to her instead of you," Clove suggested. "I wouldn't want any art featuring a naked woman in my house. It's too much pressure to make sure you always look your best."

"Right." I snickered. "You look a little pale, Clove. Are you feeling okay? I'm sure Landon will find a way to get us out of this. Don't worry."

"My stomach is upset," Clove admitted. "I feel as if I'm going to throw up. I could really use some Pepto-Bismol. Do you think they have any?"

"Chief Terry keeps some in his desk," I replied. "I've caught him drinking it during stressful cases. I think he has acid reflux."

"I can fix that." Aunt Tillie was seemingly unbothered as she studied her fingernails. "I can make a potion for him that fixes that."

"You make potions?" Ryan focused on my great-aunt. "Are you one of the witches this place brags about?"

Aunt Tillie answered without hesitation. "I am."

"You know witches aren't real, right?"

Thistle rolled her eyes and snorted. "Dude, you're here looking for aliens. You probably shouldn't crap all over witch lore — which is based in fact — when you're convinced we're about to be fed to aliens. It makes you seem like an idiot."

Ryan refused to back down. "Pretending that we're the only creatures in the universe — a universe that is expanding at a fantastic rate — is folly. Witches, on the other hand, are folk stories thought up by bored men as a way to get rid of women. I would think you'd be against something like that."

"While it's true that men throughout the ages have accused women of witchcraft as a way to rid themselves of wives they no longer wanted, that doesn't mean witchcraft isn't real," Clove argued, pressing her hand to her stomach. She really did look as if she was struggling. "I can guarantee you've seen more witches than aliens."

Ryan remained unconvinced. "Whatever."

I leaned close so I could feel Clove's forehead. She was sweating, but didn't appear to have a fever. "Are you okay?"

"I really feel sick," Clove admitted. "I think it's the stress."

"Well, you can't stay here if you're going to be sick." I got to my feet and turned toward the door, watching the agent left behind to stand guard out of the corner of my eye. "I'll get the Pepto from Chief Terry's desk."

The agent stirred when he realized I was about to leave the room. "You can't go out there, ma'am."

"Oh, I'm going out there." I refused to kowtow to these jerks for one second longer. "My cousin is sick and you have nothing you can use to hold us. I'm done here."

"Ma'am!"

I was already through the door ... and I ran directly into Landon as he calmly talked to Gibson and Chief Terry in the hallway. Instead of fear and worry reflected on his face, he was laughing.

"What are you doing?" Landon scrambled to keep me upright and make sure I didn't fall over when I did a huge double take. "Why aren't you waiting for me inside?"

My temper flared, even though I knew it wasn't a good idea. "Maybe I was worried you were being eaten by aliens. Have you ever considered that?"

"Why would aliens be eating me?"

I shrugged. "It's just something I heard."

"Let me guess, spark boy said it was a thing?" Landon dragged a restless hand through his hair. "You don't have to worry. I'm not being eaten by aliens. In fact, I think Agent Gibson and I have come to a meeting of the minds."

"Great." I couldn't muster much enthusiasm. "Clove is sick. Do you still have that Pepto in your desk, Chief Terry?"

Mirth fled his features as Chief Terry straightened. "She's sick? Are you sure she's not faking?"

"No, she's sick. She doesn't do well under stress."

"I'll grab the Pepto." Chief Terry planted his hand on my shoulder when I moved to return to the conference room. "Are you okay, sweetheart? You seem out of sorts."

"I'm tired." That was the truth. "I'm tired and I don't want to be locked in a conference room all night. I was worried you were getting in trouble, Landon. I guess that's not the case. I'll be sure to check my worry at the door next time. Oh, look, here's a door now."

Landon snagged my hand before I could storm into the conference room, pulling me against his chest and wrapping his arms around me so I couldn't escape. "Calm down. Why are you suddenly so upset?"

"Clove is sick."

"Well, I doubt she's dying. Why are you really upset?"

"Because ... I thought you were getting in trouble. But you seem as if you're enjoying yourself."

"I wouldn't go that far." Landon looked at Agent Gibson before continuing. "I have good news. Agent Gibson has something he wants to show us ... and by us, I mean you and me. That's all I could negotiate. Everyone else needs to promise they won't break the law again and then go home."

That sounded hinky. "Technically we didn't break the law," I pointed out. "You said it yourself, there were no signs warning us away. We were well within our rights."

"Which is why no charges will be filed," Landon said. "All things considered, I think we're all getting off lucky."

I wasn't convinced. "And what does Agent Gibson want to show us?"

"He won't say, but he promises it will clear up a few things."

I was all for that, still ... . "We need to take Aunt Tillie with us," I argued. "We can't cut her out of this. The others can go — and someone needs to take care of Clove — but Aunt Tillie needs to be with us."

"Are you just saying that because you don't trust her to behave herself if you're not around to watch her every move?"

That was a fair question. "Yes."

"Then Aunt Tillie can come." Landon held up a hand to quiet Agent Gibson before he could argue. "Trust me. It's not worth fighting with her. She'll make you cry before it's all said and done. We'll be better off bringing her along."

"Fine." Gibson didn't look happy. "I'm not sure this is a good idea, but I'll agree to it just to put this behind us."

"Fair enough." Landon nodded as he stroked his hands over my back. "The sooner we get this handled, the better off everybody will be."

"That's the only reason I suggested this in the first place."

ALIEN INSPIRATION

> I want to be that Sigourney Weaver character Ripley when I grow up. She kicks alien butt. If that doesn't work, I want to be Cinderella. All she has to do is find a man and then everything ends up perfect. She gets a good world with zero work. Who doesn't want that? Yeah, I take it back. I want to be a princess and not an alien fighter. Forget what I said.
> **Clove talks future choices**

TWENTY

JUST WHEN YOU THOUGHT IT WAS SAFE TO GO BACK TO THE INN.

*C*love was happy to be cut out of our excursion. Thistle was hard to read, but didn't put up a fight. Whatever Gibson was about to show us, she knew we would relate in great detail ... once he left town.

Chief Terry drove, insisting that he needed his own vehicle, and Landon sat in the front with him. That left me to sit in the back with Aunt Tillie. She wasn't particularly perturbed about the new development.

"I bet he's going to show us an alien." Aunt Tillie rubbed her hands together as she peered out the window. "I can't wait. I'm going to name him Spock and we're going to have grand adventures."

I had my doubts. "He's not going to show us an alien."

"Definitely not," Landon agreed, his eyes focused out the windshield. "I think he's going to show us something else."

"What?" I whispered.

"Whatever crashed in that field."

Hmm. I hadn't even considered that. It made sense, though. "Do you think he'll talk to me on the record when he's done?"

Landon shrugged. "I wouldn't count on it."

That's what I was afraid of.

IT TURNED OUT LANDON was right. Gibson, who was in the vehicle ahead of us, pulled into the parking lot of an abandoned lumberyard. It was located between Hemlock Cove and a neighboring town, and I never once thought to check there for anything, let alone the big truck parked in the lot.

"Do you think it's in the back?" I asked Landon as he helped me out of the truck. The day was starting to catch up with me and I felt weary.

"I think it is." Landon pressed a quick kiss to my forehead. "We need to keep watch over Aunt Tillie. Gibson will lose his cool pretty quickly if she runs her usual shtick on him."

"I think he kind of deserves to put up with her."

"And I think I want to escape this with nothing but a reprimand on my record."

I gripped his hand before he could walk ahead of me. "How much trouble are you in?" I naturally assumed when I saw them talking in the hallway that everything was okay. Apparently, that wasn't true. "Maybe I could talk to Gibson and tell him it was my fault."

Landon chuckled as he shook his head. "I don't think it's going to be a big deal. Even if it is, I don't want you worrying about it. I made a choice to go into the woods with you tonight. I don't regret that choice."

"But ... it's not fair to you."

"Life isn't fair, Bay. I'm fine with how things turned out. It could've been much worse. I don't want you worrying about this, okay? You'll make yourself sick like Clove, and that's the last thing I want."

"Yeah, that was weird, huh?" I straightened my shoulders. "She's always been bad under pressure — she once threw up on Chief Terry's shoes when he caught us drinking by the lake when we were teenagers — but she seems even shakier than normal tonight."

"She'll be okay." Landon gave my hand a reassuring squeeze. "A good night's sleep will make everything better."

"I hope so."

I moved with Landon to stand at the back of the truck, my eyes tracking to my left when Aunt Tillie appeared at my elbow. She seemed excited — unusually so — and she practically vibrated with energy as she watched one of the agents move to the back of the truck.

"Here it is. We're finally going to see an alien. Did I tell you I'm going to name it Spock?"

"It's not an alien," Landon snapped, his world-famous cool slipping. "Why do you think it's an alien?"

"Because that's the only thing that makes sense."

As if on cue, Agent Gibson appeared out of the darkness. He'd clearly heard Aunt Tillie's statement and he almost looked amused as he made a clucking sound with his tongue. "I think you're about to be extremely disappointed."

"I don't think so." Aunt Tillie inclined her chin toward the door. "Show me."

"Fine. You asked for it." Gibson gestured for his man to open the back of the truck. It took a moment, and the metal sound was jarring when the door rolled up. Three agents fixed flashlight beams on the opening, and I had to squint to make out what we were looking at.

"What is that?"

"It's a flying saucer," Aunt Tillie announced as she stepped forward. "Has anyone checked the cockpit? The alien is probably in the cockpit."

"If there was an alien in there, he'd be burned to a crisp," I argued, wrinkling my nose at the sight of the charred hulk that might have been an aircraft of some sort at one time. "There's clearly no alien in there. In fact ... ." I leaned forward so I could read the lettering on the side of the wreckage. "What does that say?"

"Aero something or other," Landon replied. "I think it's a farm drone."

"That's exactly what it is." Gibson folded his arms over his chest as he watched our reactions. "It was an unmanned prototype. It was meant to disperse chemicals over fields, which would essentially cut down on the time growers have to spend fighting pests. It's a new innovation ... and clearly they haven't worked out the kinks."

"But ... ." Disappointment washed over me. That was even more boring than a government drone training.

"Why all the fuss if it was simply a farm drone?" Landon challenged. "Why not just tell us from the start?"

"Believe it or not, the technology on this thing is classified," Gibson replied. "It started out as a missile drone and was adapted for another purpose. If the technology were to get out, that would be bad."

"Still, you made a big deal out of it," I persisted. "If you'd simply explained that it was a farming drone, nobody would have cared."

"No, *you* wouldn't have cared," Gibson corrected. "Competitors interested in farming drones would've descended on the area to steal the technology."

"Yes, that would've been a terrifying two people," I muttered. "Are there really competitors who would care enough to travel here?"

"Agriculture is a growing field and people are definitely interested in getting a leg up," Gibson supplied. "The technology on this drone is not in the public domain. We had to make sure that we accounted for every piece of machinery that we could. We also needed to spray a chemical that rendered the pesticide on the drone inert. Most of the pesticide burned away, but it was still a concern."

"That explains why you were conducting the grid search," I said. "You were looking for tiny fragments."

"As it stands, that field is clean. There is nothing there other than charred earth, which will be gone in a few weeks thanks to the time of year. Nature always reclaims what is torn asunder, and this will be no different."

"Huh." I rubbed my cheek, annoyed. "I don't get it. What about the people who were acting differently?"

Gibson furrowed his brow. "What people are you referring to?"

"Mrs. Little, for starters. She and Doris were acting dippy this afternoon. I swear they were stalking me outside the newspaper."

"Oh, that's probably my fault," Aunt Tillie interjected. "Did they say what they were looking for?"

"No. Why? What did you do to them?"

"I didn't technically do anything to them," Aunt Tillie replied. "They might believe that I was spying on them because I thought they were aliens. Oh, and also that I may have put a sparkly halter top on a certain fiberglass unicorn, although good luck proving that in court. That thing is an eyesore. It should be banned from town."

"I knew you were the one who put that bra on the unicorn," Chief Terry groused. "I was going to track you down and make you confess but I had other things to focus on. When Margaret came to the station I sent her to The Whistler, Bay. I was trying to distract her and said I thought Tillie was hanging around with you."

I searched my memory of the incident. "But they were both acting so odd."

"*Invasion of the Body Snatchers* odd?" Landon teased.

I refused to meet his gaze. "That doesn't explain why Mrs. Little was acting so strangely the other day. She couldn't even remember my name."

"I talked to her about that," Chief Terry said. "I only asked her because you seemed so worried. She had a dentist appointment the day after the crash. She needed bridgework done and it was painful ... so they loaded her up on nitrous."

No, that couldn't be right. "She shouldn't have been wandering around under those conditions."

"Yes, well, you tell her that," Chief Terry suggested. "She doesn't like listening to me when I say anything of the sort."

My frustration bubbled over. "So you're saying that I allowed Aunt Tillie to work me into a frenzy about aliens even though it was basically a crop duster that went down in a field ... and it was pesticide that burned that guy's hands, not alien goo. Is that what you're saying?"

Gibson shrugged. "Pretty much."

"This sucks."

Landon slid an arm around my shoulders and chuckled, the sound warm and throaty as he shook his head. "It definitely sucks. I feel like an idiot."

"I don't." Chief Terry refused to back down. "If you'd told us from the start what was going on, Agent Gibson, we could have nipped this hysteria in the bud. You didn't, so that's on you."

"I agree that it would've been better for everyone concerned to tell the truth from the start, but I was under strict orders," Gibson argued. "It's not my fault that this happened. Had you two followed orders and minded your own business, none of this would've happened tonight."

"Oh, it still would've happened," Landon argued. "It simply would've gone down a different way. You're actually lucky I was with them. Things could've gotten out of control otherwise."

"I would hate to think things could get worse," Gibson said. "Still, it's not the end of the world. Now you know."

"Yeah, now we know," I echoed, resting my head against Landon's chest. "Aliens would've been a lot more fun."

"I know." Landon brushed his lips against my cheek as he pulled me in for a hug. "Still, nobody died, and Aunt Tillie never got a shot off. It could have been so much worse."

He had a point.

"Speaking of Bessie, I want my gun back," Aunt Tillie announced. "I've decided to rename her, by the way. I'm going to call her Gibson because she's a real ass—."

Chief Terry slapped his hand over Aunt Tillie's mouth. "I think we're done here. We'll be on our way. You can just leave Tillie's gun in my office when you head out. I'll make sure it gets back where it's supposed to be."

Gibson nodded curtly. "Of course. Again, I'm sorry to disappoint you."

"Somehow I think we'll get over it."

IT WAS ALMOST MIDNIGHT before Landon and I returned to the guesthouse. Once free of Gibson's disdainful glare, Aunt Tillie turned into a ranting machine. Chief Terry had to take us out to Hollow Creek to reclaim Landon's Explorer, so she had plenty of time to make her opinion known.

In the end, she decided that the crop duster story was cover and the government was trying to cover up the beginning stages of an alien invasion. I was so exhausted by the time she hopped out of the vehicle and headed toward the inn that I could barely keep my eyes open.

"Tonight didn't go as I expected," I said as Landon put the Explorer in park and killed the engine. "I thought for sure we were going to find something fantastical, maybe even otherworldly."

"Aunt Tillie was with us," Landon pointed out as I shoved open my door. "It doesn't get much more otherworldly than that."

"Ha, ha." I looked up and stared at the sky as Landon joined me in front of the Explorer. "Do you think aliens exist?"

Landon followed my gaze. "I don't know. Do you?"

"I think that the universe is too vast for us to be the only ones," I replied. "I mean ... how sad would that be? All those planets ... and stars ... and space. How could we be the only ones?"

"I guess that's basically how I feel, too," Landon acknowledged. "That doesn't mean I think aliens are landing in Hemlock Cove and looking for people to probe."

"I hope they probe Mrs. Little when they land." My gaze turned dark. "I'm serious. I thought there was something significantly wrong with her ... even more than normal. Turns out nitrous makes her likable. I didn't see that coming."

Landon snickered, genuinely amused. "I don't think any of us saw that coming. Still, I'd rather blame nitrous than aliens. Do you know how much paperwork would be associated with aliens?"

"You're a funny guy."

"I try."

I slipped into his embrace so he could help me ward off the cold. "I never believed it was aliens," I said finally. "I only let Aunt Tillie think I believed because ... well ... she seemed to need it."

"Uh-huh." Landon clearly wasn't convinced. "I'm glad you didn't believe it was aliens. I would have to worry about you otherwise."

"You don't need to worry." I felt foolish enough that I was convinced I wouldn't bring up aliens again for years. "I'm just glad it's over."

"Me, too." Landon swayed back and forth. "I know we talked about a bath, but how would you feel if we went straight to bed and saved the bath for tomorrow?"

"Sounds like a plan to me." I pulled back and tipped up my chin. "I'm glad you didn't get into too much trouble."

"It would've been worth it regardless. I like it when we're on the same team."

"You and me both. I ... ." I trailed off as a low humming filled the air. The hair on the back of my neck stood on end. "What the ... ?"

Landon clutched me tighter as he swiveled quickly and stared in the direction of Potter's Field. A bright light hovered over the field. I had no idea what was happening, no basis for comparison, but I knew the light wasn't naturally occurring.

"I thought Gibson said they were done in the field," I said, my eyes widening as the light drifted higher and a revolving circle of smaller lights started spinning unbelievably fast. It didn't look like a vessel ... or a flying saucer. It definitely didn't look like a crop duster. What it did look like, I couldn't say. I had no frame of reference for it. "Do you think they went back for some reason?"

Landon swallowed hard. "I don't know." He put his hands over my head to shelter me as the light moved even higher before suddenly picking up speed and streaking across the sky, leaving a faint rainbow of glittering light behind. It was gone in a split-second, leaving Potter's Field dark again. It happened so fast I almost wondered if I'd imagined it.

"Landon?" It took me a few moments to find my voice. I wasn't sure he could hear me over the pounding of my heart.

"What, sweetie?"

"I think we should go to bed. We're clearly both exhausted."

"That's exactly what I was thinking." Landon gave me a little shove toward the guesthouse. "Don't ever bring this up again, Bay. I don't want to encourage Aunt Tillie."

"Bring what up? I have no idea what you're talking about."

"Good girl." Landon dug into the pocket of his shirt and came back with five pieces of candy, remnants of what Aunt Tillie threw at him earlier in the evening. He tossed it onto the yard before following me to the door. "It couldn't hurt," he said finally at my questioning stare.

"Right." I pushed my key in the lock. "Do you think ... ?"

"I think it's time for bed." Landon was firm. "No more adventures tonight."

"Okay, but I was only going to ask if aliens like bacon. If so, we should probably stop by the grocery store and stock up tomorrow. You know, in case there's a shortage or something."

"I like the way your mind works."

"Right back at you."

Printed in Great Britain
by Amazon